MW01148367

PASSIONATE PLUME AWARD, Best Erotic Western

EPIC AWARD- WINNER, Best Historical Western, Best Erotic Western

EPIC AWARD- FINALIST, Best Historical Erotic Romance

THE GOLDEN NIB AWARD- Best Erotic Historical Western "Books that Knock Our Socks Off"-Miz Love Loves Books.

What the Reviewers are saying about the series...

"...tantalizing tale, true historical attitudes, intriguing plot, sizzling romance...Gem Sivad is quickly becoming one of my favorite storytellers!" Dogwood~ Long and Short Reviews

"...I was mesmerized from the beginning. The scenes were action-packed and...quite erotic...the sensuality sizzling and very, very frequent..." Brenda~The Romance Studio Reviews

"...The explosions of their sexual encounters are the stuff of dreams..." Alberta~ Manic Readers

Published by Gem Sivad, LLC

Editor: L. Smithers
Cover Design: Kristian Norris
Sivad, Gem (2016-05-13).
Gem Sivad LLC. Kindle Edition.
ISBN-13: 978-1533607669
ISBN-10: 1533607664

Trademarks Acknowledgement

The author acknowledges the trademarked status and trademark owners of the following wordmarks mentioned in this work of fiction:

Colt .45: Colt's Patent Fire Arms Manufacturing Co., Inc.

Winchester Repeating Arms: Olin Corporation

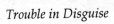
Trouble in Disguise

Prologue

August, 1885

Deacon McCallister lay face-down. Spread-eagled on the packed dirt, his arms and legs anchored by stakes driven into the ground, he squinted blearily through sweat and tears he couldn't control.

Captured earlier because of his own stupidity, he'd been tortured, suffering silently under Alistair Pettigrew's flaying knife as the outlaw cut thin strips of skin from his back. Now, though it was still morning, the heat of the sun burned his damaged flesh and he shuddered as insects discovered the feast.

One of the gang's camp followers had decided to have fun too. He wanted to scream, but he strangled the sound and lay unmoving in the dirt while the woman crouched next to him, layering honey over the raw wounds on his back. The sweet balm melted, soothing the flayed flesh. But, making Deacon comfortable wasn't her intent.

"Come see how the ants love his taste," she coaxed Pettigrew.

Deacon's stomach knotted, anticipating more agony as the outlaw leader joined her. When Pettigrew kicked dirt, sending a cascade of stones over the raw wounds, Deacon's breath caught in his chest and he locked his jaw to stifle a moan. After he'd faded to a near unconscious state, the shock of water dribbling down his face revived him.

"Stop that. I want the sonofabitch thirsty," Pettigrew ordered the woman.

"If he passes out, sugar, you'll miss the fun of seeing his pain." Regardless of her purpose for delivering it, the water trickled to his mouth, moistened his lips, and cleared Deacon's head. Squatting the way she was, the woman's dress had bunched high enough above her knee to show the top of the boot and the knife sheathed there.

"Let me just get that spot on the far side and paint him up good. Then you and me'll have us some fun." Instead of standing and walking around his body, the woman leaned over Deacon. Her skirts fell over his arm, covering the stake that tethered his right hand. Her knee leaned so close to Deacon, his knuckles brushed the knife handle.

He pulled against the leather strip that bound his wrist. His stiff, almost unresponsive fingers, fumbled and came up empty. Any moment he expected her to call out and expose his actions, but she angled herself farther across his body, slathering more honey on his back, indifferent to his desperate grope. He wrapped his fingers around the handle, but he couldn't slide the knife from the boot.

"That ought to bring the critters on real fast." She sat back on her heels, releasing the blade into his hand as she moved. She admired her work, her skirts still covering the upper right stake and blessedly hiding the knife he'd secured. Wasting no time, he slid the blade between his skin and the rawhide binding him.

"You like watchin' 'em die slow, don't you?" Pettigrew praised her, and even Deacon could hear the surge of lust in the other man's voice. Evidently more interested at the moment in rutting than torturing, the outlaw suddenly jerked the woman to her feet. "Gets ya kinda juiced up, don't it, girl?"

"Sure does." The woman laughed, plastering herself to the outlaw, and indicating her approval of

Pettigrew's idea of romance. There was no way to hide the knife clutched in Deacon's hand which her standing had exposed. Deacon tried to keep from slitting his own wrist as he desperately sawed at the leather tied so tight it cut into his skin.

He sliced through one strip and started on the other when the outlaw groaned and fell to the ground. Panicked, Deacon tried to make the blade cut faster so he could get loose and defend himself.

But the woman remained draped across the fallen man, sealing his mouth with hers as he arched, grunted and then slumped under her. The woman rolled off Pettigrew, revealing a different knife sticking from his chest heart-high. Wasting no time, she pulled that blade free and crouched by Deacon's feet, severing the ties binding his ankles.

"Beau sent me. I've got a horse waiting and we're leaving. I'll need your help."

As soon as his legs were freed, Deacon struggled to his knees and gazed at the young woman. White-blonde hair cascaded down her back, oddly contrasting with the dark brows and lashes accenting fiercely demanding gray eyes.

"Put this on. You're about the same size." The soft edges of her drawl mixed with a harsher twang as she gave him orders. She handed Deacon the outlaw's black hat. "The others have their backs turned so as not to see you get carved up and me fucked. Don't count on that lasting if they get curious."

Even in his desperate state, her crude words and rough accent jarred in his mind. They didn't match her face. Nevertheless, too blurred by his hurting to do much thinking, he waited for her to direct his moves.

She removed Pettigrew's shirt, rolling him over so he lay on the spot just vacated by Deacon, then kicked the body's legs apart, mimicking the shape that had lain there before.

She worked so fast, Deacon barely realized what she'd done before she focused on him again. Sliding his arm around her shoulders, she lifted him to his feet, half carrying and half dragging him toward the bushes and rocks beyond.

"It'll take a damn miracle to get out of this fix."

His growled opinion made her snort.

"Lucky ya got one then, McCallister. Now get a move on."

"How many wanteds?" he muttered, trying to get his feet moving faster than a slow shuffle.

"Enough to make Christmas right promising this year," she answered.

Deacon had counted more than a half-dozen outlaws when he'd ridden into camp. He didn't think the woman had a chance in hell of getting out with or without him. But if rival bounty hunter Beau Beauregard was helping her, that might not be the case. Since Deacon was on his feet and it looked as if he might have a chance at surviving, he didn't question the possibility further.

"Hey!" The shout warned them they'd been discovered.

"Ketchum, get him." She shouted the order and kept moving, ignoring the outlaw behind them.

"Where's Beauregard?" Deacon muttered, grasping the one thing that made sense. Knowing that the kid had orchestrated the rescue, gave Deacon hope. He might make it through the day alive. He could hear the sound of a snarling beast behind him and that was additional incentive to believe.

"Up you go," she murmured, seemingly unafraid as she faced Beauregard's pinto. The animal stood quietly as the woman boosted Deacon to the back of the saddle seat. She mounted in front of him. "Wrap your arms around my middle and hang on."

"I won't let go. Ride hard, hellcat," he growled in her ear. He didn't know how she pulled it off other than sheer guts. He wasn't any use other than clinging like a limpet to her back.

Their mount took off at a dead run and the woman knee-guided the horse while she held a gun in each hand, clearing a path with bullets as they raced through the main camp heading for the corridor leading out of the canyon. Behind them, Deacon heard a wolf snarling, horses streamed past them in the granite corridor, and then they were out.

He started to slide and grappled for a better hold, clutching a plump breast in his fist.

"Hang on to something substantial, ya dang fool." She holstered one gun and grabbed his hand, moving it to her waist. Then she reached back, pressing his shoulder and attempting to shift him closer to her body. "Dadblamed honey's slippery," she complained.

"You painted me with the mess, what do you expect?" Deacon focused on their sporadic conversation, trying to keep himself from passing out. "You owe me for the honey." He didn't know what else to say so he hung his head over her shoulder and complained.

"Mister, honey's a mite dear where I come from. *You* owe *me*. It'll take me six ways to Sunday to replace my stash."

Even confused by the agony of his back, the woman's drawled answer perplexed Deacon. He held on to a woman's body but heard Beauregard speak. Deacon figured the pain had just been too much and sent him to crazy land.

Chapter One

Three months later, Hell's Half Acre

Deacon McCallister mounted wide, curving steps leading to the grand entrance of the Southern-styled plantation house. Among its mediocre copycats, the building at the end of Rusk Street made an impressive statement. Windows decorating the first and second levels viewed the world with amber eyes as afternoon lamps glowed behind filmy curtains.

Smoke drifting above each of the chimneys indicated fires had been lit inside to stave off the chill of the dreary day. The weather was unusually cold for October and Deacon appreciated the warmth of his leather duster although its weight irritated the new scars on his back.

He was here because Hiram Potter, the Eclipse sheriff, had asked him to check on Beau Beauregard.

"I got a wire this week. The kid's in Hell's Half Acre hunting a counterfeiter. I kicked up a fuss about him working alone after what happened to you so he's keeping me posted as to his whereabouts."

Deacon didn't need the oblique reminder that without Beauregard's recent rescue he'd be dead. Ungrateful though he might be, he was more interested in meeting the woman who'd risked her life for him. Gulling as it was, Beauregard was the only one who knew her.

Hiram evidently thought Beauregard in danger, stumbling around somewhere in Fort Worth. Deacon sorely doubted it. But he had additional incentive to find the young bounty hunter since Beau's trail intersected with that of the fake money. The McCallisters had been stung by the counterfeiters along with half the Territory.

This is a waste of time. There's no way they'd let that brat inside. Picturing the lanky, half-grown youth in his floppy hat and buckskins, Deacon let his gaze sweep over the elegant edifice before him.

When the kid was on the hunt, he had a nose like a bloodhound, but it didn't seem probable that the owner of this establishment was his quarry. Nevertheless, Deacon continued climbing the steps, intent on reaching the door before the guards watching him from their patrol posts decided he wasn't fit for entrance either.

Deacon reached the top of the steps and faced the ornate entry. At his first knock, the door swung open and he was greeted by a doorman ushering him into the Pleasure Dome, one of the premiere whorehouses in Fort Worth, Texas.

"Lydia in?" he asked gruffly, avoiding the gaze of the butler as he stared at the lavish décor. Silently the doorkeeper escorted him to the sitting room, waved him to a seat and left him alone to wait for the owner of the brothel. After only a few moments, Lydia joined him.

"Robert," Lydia said, flashing him a dimpled smile and holding her hands out as she entered the room. "When Calvin announced your presence, I couldn't believe it. It's been too long." If one didn't know better, Lydia would be described as a sweetly refined gentlewoman. Deacon knew better. Her discreetly flirtatious manner covered the mind of a shop owner assessing a customer.

The infamous madam had been childhood friends with Deacon's wife, Annie. The two women hadn't visited often and Deacon had met Lydia no more than a half-dozen times before Annie's death. After he'd hunted down his wife's murderers, severed ties with the church and become a bounty hunter instead of a preacher, Lydia had invited him to become her lover and partner in a brothel.

He'd declined both offers, but when Annie's old friend opened her establishment in Hell's Half Acre, Deacon sometimes visited. He steadfastly declined intimacy with Lydia and made it a point to keep his couplings emotionless, never bedding the same paid companion twice. His use of prostitutes shamed him and he didn't visit often. When he did, he paid well and marked his weakness as another smudge on his character.

He took in the lush elegance of mahogany furniture and silk curtains surrounding the madam. "Business seems to be flourishing."

Lydia nodded proudly. She'd elevated decadence to a new level. Every suite was fitted with a fireplace, imported carpets and a grand-sized bed with sumptuous decorations. The crème de la crème in each was the porcelain bathing tub fit for a king.

As a madam in a dissolute town where sin was a common commodity, she'd set her place apart from the other bawdy houses by providing refined women with poise and beauty and showcasing them against a backdrop of genteel luxury. Her competitors had scoffed at her excesses, claiming she'd never make enough money to cover her costs. Apparently they'd been wrong.

She'd imported a chef famous for his culinary skills and more than one politician had been known to dine at the Pleasure Dome, eating delicious cuisine in the hall lit by crystal chandeliers. Lydia's services were circumspect, exotic and expensive.

Deacon wasn't here for the food but socializing with the infamous madam was part of the ritual of receiving information, another commodity that Lydia provided for her customers. When he visited, he always brought a little gossip and a few facts she might sell or give to another — nothing that might damage his own interests but might someday further her own.

He figured most of her customers did the same thing, feeding her tidbits that didn't affect them. Like an elegant spider, Lydia sat spinning straw into gilded treasure in the midst of her beautiful Hell's Half Acre web.

Deacon gazed at the subtle but expensive décor and wondered if Lydia had spun fool's gold to pay for it. He pulled out two fake bank notes, laying the ten beside the hundred on the table next to her.

"Really, Robert, don't be crude. I'm not a store clerk collecting money." Lydia flushed and frowned.

"Counterfeit," he said and leaned forward, pointing at the bills. "I thought you might want to know more like those two are being circulated here in Fort Worth."

"Dear God, show me how to tell the real from the fake." Shock replaced anger in her expression as she stared at the bills, waiting for his help in determining the phony money.

Lydia's response of genuine horror left little doubt that if the Pleasure Dome was being used as a conduit, the owner knew nothing about it.

"The banks are checking bills." He pointed out the serial number on each and explained how to differentiate between the real and the false.

"This makes everything that much more difficult," she complained and wasted no time devising a means to counteract the threat to her profits. "I'll have to have each escort checking money now."

"You need to pass on the information." He nodded at the bills. It was understood that she'd alert businessmen and politicians alike. Her reach extended to the inner chambers of the rich and powerful.

He hesitated. He should be on his way. By warning Lydia, he'd done his duty to Fort Worth commerce and fulfilled part of his goal. He wasn't going to find his young competitor among the Pleasure Dome's elite clientele.

Deacon gazed around the room, weighing the pros and cons of staying. Inhaling the scent of decadence, he decided his good deed of finding Beauregard could wait.

"I'm going to need a room for the night." He pocketed the two counterfeit bills and decided to further his stay.

"Only the best for you, Robert." Lydia stood, smoothing nonexistent wrinkles from her skirt before heading for the door. "I'll have Calvin escort you upstairs when your bath is prepared and your suite ready."

"I'll dine before I go up," he answered. It would be interesting to see who was in Lydia's fancy dining hall.

"No, you won't. Don't forget in your zeal to catch criminals that my establishment is neutral territory." She showed him the ruthless face of the

Pleasure Dome's madam and said shrewdly, "I'll have your dinner delivered. Enjoy your stay, Robert."

Deacon's interest sharpened at her determination to keep him away from her other guests.

She started to leave then paused. "You've certainly saved me from possible problems. I'll send someone special to you tonight." Her message was clear. *Eat, drink, debauch at will. But stay away from my customers.*

"Not necessary," he answered as she closed the door. He wasn't sure that she'd heard or if he wanted her to. He thought about the ribbon of scars on his back, still pink and tender. It wasn't a sight he particularly wanted to share.

Lydia promised someone special every time he visited. He suspected that was a pat phrase she used on her patrons. When the door clicked shut, Deacon knew he had two choices.

He could prowl through the gaming hells and saloons in Fort Worth and spend the night looking for Beauregard or he could sit tight and let himself be escorted upstairs. Since exploring the brothel was unlikely given the many security guards Lydia had patrolling her house, staying overnight was an indulgence.

The skin on his back itched, his muscles ached and the spicy scent of something cooking in the kitchen made his belly rumble. He focused on the main reason why he should stay. A long soak in one of Lydia's tubs would feel good. As if conjured by his thoughts, she popped back into the room.

"I'm afraid Calvin has left his post to smoke for the last time." Lydia wore a frown as she fussed about her butler. The expression made her appear years older.

"As you well know, Robert, I cannot tolerate the smell of tobacco. It ruins the carpets and fouls the air."

He knew Lydia's rules as did every other customer ten steps through her front door. It appeared she wasn't fussing about tobacco as much as her butler though.

"If he wasn't such a pretty boy I would already have fired him." Doorman absent or not, Lydia had no intentions of turning Deacon loose to roam.

"Benjamin will see you upstairs." Benjamin was a bruiser dressed in a fine suit tailored to fit smoothly across muscles and concealed weapons.

Deacon remained silent as they climbed the broad sweep of stairs leading to the suites above. Upon arrival, he handed the escort a stack of greenbacks, which the man refused.

"Lydia says you're her guest this visit. Dinner will be delivered at midnight. Enjoy your stay at the Pleasure Dome."

Deacon waited until the other man disappeared down the steps. Then he fitted the key into the lock, entered and relocked the door before he faced the woman who'd been sent to entertain him.

Shock coursed through him. Lydia's promise of someone *special* had for once been fulfilled. Deacon crossed the room and stood before the waiting girl. Women rarely reached above chest high on Deacon since, even barefoot, he dwarfed most men. But his night's companion met his gaze without tilting her head or craning her neck.

Sooty lashes framed gray eyes flecked with silver, making her appearance strangely exotic. Charcoal brows contrasted with both her pale skin and the white-blonde hair hanging in a silken mane down her back.

"You work for Lydia?" His astonished words were out before he could stop himself.

"Tonight I work for you." She laughed and touched his sleeve.

Surely she remembered him. But she didn't mention that the last time they'd met, he'd been staked out flat, with a maniac carving strips of flesh from his back. Was it possible she'd never gotten a look at his face?

That was the first surprise. Her clothes or lack thereof was his second. Usually Lydia had her girls decked out in transparent costumes that left nothing to the imagination.

This woman wore a ruffled white shirt buttoned from shirttail to neck. It revealed little but what he could see made his breath catch in his throat. His gaze trailed upward, enjoying the shape of her bare feet, defined calves, not quite bony knees and pale columns of sculpted muscles. His gaze stalled on the tail of the shirt where it touched the top of her thighs.

She brushed her hands down her front as if trying to make the material cover more of her. The gesture served only to mold the fabric to her plump breasts, marking the white shirt with dents from the stiff peaks of her taut nipples.

She glanced at her chest and unexpectedly chuckled, the husky sound making its way straight to Deacon's groin. He forgot about his mission to save Beauregard and ended all thoughts of spending the night alone.

Matter-of-factly she raised her arms to divide the thick mane hanging down her back. When she pulled two thick strands over her shoulders, her shirt pulled taut, displaying puckered nubs. He wanted her.

"I need to clean up," he said abruptly. She gestured at the tub in the middle of the floor. He shook his head. "Shave first, then bathe."

He scrubbed his hands and then made short work of lathering his face. He didn't want to get dirty prints on the white material when he removed it. Excitement rippled through him. "Unbutton your shirt so I can look at you while I scrape off this beard."

Absently he palmed the soap, rubbing it into lather while he surveyed her. The pale skin and light hair should have made her appear drab or dull but instead they served as a creamy landscape framing each vivid splash of color in her features.

Apricot blush tinted her cheeks as she obediently reached for the buttons closest to the bottom. Long tapered fingers unfastened the first four and stopped. The sight of her calloused palm and strong wrist startled him but he forgot about it when he glimpsed the soft nest of curls on her mound.

His glance traveled over the ruffles on the linen shirt past the full swell of unfettered breasts, up the elegant line of her neck. He paused and watched the tip of her pink tongue wet ruby lips. His gaze continued upward until he stared into her eyes. He'd been wrong. They weren't gray but dark silver, the color of pewter. Laugh lines crinkled at the corners as she lifted a brow inquiringly.

"You don't remember me?" He tensed, waiting.

"Of course I remember you," she laughed, her tone husky when she added, "Beau said you needed rescued so there was no way out of it. You owe me a honeycomb. I'm glad to see I didn't waste it doctoring you."

"You let Beauregard persuade you to go into that camp. That was crazy."

"Well now," she drawled agreeably, "we could talk about that. Or — we could play."

It had been a long time since Deacon had played. A growl of pleasure rumbled in his chest. Though his hands were covered in lather, he touched the ruffled shirt's neck, ran his finger down the front placket and paused when her breasts swelled on either side of his fingers.

"To here," he said, leaving a wet mark that clearly defined where she could stop. He resumed shaving, staring at the reflection of his jaw in the mirror instead of at her. Deacon concentrated on keeping his hand from trembling as he scraped away dark whiskers.

"Want me to use that on you?" She gestured at the straight razor, stepping closer to him so he could see her reflection.

The button marking the wet spot he'd left in the middle of the shirt kept it from falling open. Lust roared through him.

"No, you do sloppy work." He rinsed the razor in the bowl of water, flicking the excess water from it before slicing through the threads holding the last button in place. "You missed one."

She leaned against the dresser and shifted her stance, displaying long, strong thighs covered in pale satiny skin—and the juncture between them. Deacon flipped apart the shirt, revealing the high full breasts. A drop of water flicked from his hand to slide down her pearl-white flesh.

Her body was spare, without the usual softness or voluptuous curves he'd come to expect on a woman. Though her arms and shoulders were subtly defined by muscle, nothing on her body suggested excess other than the full bottom lip presenting him with a wickedly plump promise of sin—and the decadence of her breasts.

He held her gaze and cupped the rounded globes that defied the angles and planes of the rest of her. Need clawed inside him as the exquisite silk of her skin caressed his rough palms. Besides bringing his cock to life, she had a coltish grace that stirred a deeper part of him.

Instead of clipping his beard, he'd shaved it completely off. He felt almost naked without his facial hair.

"Where you shaved, your skin's as smooth as a baby's bottom." She leaned closer, stroking the back of her hand along his jaw and he turned his head, capturing her fingers in his mouth.

His reward was a startled hiss and goose bumps chasing over her skin. He kept her from removing her fingers and sucked on two of them, teasing them hard enough to make her nipples stand in stiff peaks. She moaned a husky sound of desire and swayed nearer, brushing against his shirt with her naked breasts. Relinquishing her fingers, he splashed water on his face before blotting the excess on a towel.

He wanted to close his lips around her nub, lave and suckle it until she whimpered and worry it with his teeth and tongue until she screamed and demanded more. As if she read his mind, she stepped back slightly, letting the sides of her shirt come together to hide her treasure.

"Your bath's ready now." Her hand trembled slightly as she pointed at the tub. Steam rose from the half-filled porcelain device that was big enough to accommodate both him and his companion.

Deacon grunted in appreciation. A woven screen decorated with pictures of exotic birds stood to the side, ready to give privacy if so desired.

"You can talk to me while I get rid of this layer of dust." He dropped his hand to his shirt. "I'm pretty ripe from the trail," he warned her.

Their play during his shave had eased the awkwardness between two strangers but suddenly he was self-conscious. Before he'd fumbled open the second button on his shirt she took over.

"I've smelled worse," she assured him, unbuckling and laying aside his gun belt before returning to the front of his pants. His swollen cock pushed against the denim material, making it hard to free the buttons from their slots. She bit her lip, concentrating on her task and avoiding his stare.

As he examined his paid companion, her cheeks flushed and had he not understood that she was a prostitute and experienced at the game, he would have said she was shy. As it was, he acknowledged Lydia's claim. His night's entertainment was special. She knew how to feign innocence.

After she mastered his buttons, she knelt next to his feet and his cock ached at the thought of her mouth on him. Obediently he steadied himself by holding her shoulder, admiring the silken length of thigh exposed to his view as she removed his boots and socks.

As soon as he stood in his bare feet, he freed his cock and stripped off the dusty denims. She remained crouched on the floor when he stood naked before her, his member a rigid lance begging to be buried between her legs—or lips. He stopped her when she lifted her hand as if to touch it.

"Not yet. Let me get clean first so we can both enjoy it." Hastily, before he succumbed to lust, he stepped into the tub, dipping below the water and hiding his back. She surprised him again when she pressed him forward in the tub, inspecting his scars. They were healed but still tender welts running from his lower back to his shoulders. Silently, she picked up a sponge and began to bathe him.

"Pretty hair," she murmured, soaping his head and kneading his scalp. He leaned into her ministrations, closing his eyes and shedding the weight of the world as she rubbed away the knots of tension at the back of his skull and then stroked lower, massaging his shoulders. He groaned, savoring bliss.

After she'd thoroughly rubbed and scrubbed, she popped open the drain and rinsed suds from his hair as the dirty water emptied.

"Hand me a towel," he said gruffly. "I can take it from here." His cock stood rigid between his thighs, reminding him why he'd prolonged his visit to the Pleasure Dome. Instead of handing him a towel, she blotted the excess drops from his head before leaning over his shoulder, closing the drain, and turning on the water to refill the tub.

"I favor a bath myself," she explained when he looked at her in surprise.

He was ready for bed sports himself. She had him so hot he thought the new water might start boiling. But she'd earned the right to be in charge. He stayed in the tub. The sound of her shirt hitting the floor accompanied her slide in behind him. She gathered him in an embrace, pressing her breasts against his back and holding on to him as water inched higher, surrounding them in a pool of warmth.

"Ease on back and relax." She was showing a surprising bossy streak but under the circumstances, Deacon let it slide. When he lay with his head nestled against her shoulder, drifting mindlessly in a fog of pleasure, she wrapped her legs around his waist, locking her feet and holding him captive. "Gotcha," she said as if he was her prisoner.

Except for the ache in his shaft, Deacon couldn't remember ever being so comfortable. He repositioned her hand, moving it from where it stroked his chest, guiding it to his groin and the rigid length of his arousal. His cock grew harder and her hand trembled under his.

She rode into an outlaw camp and saved my sorry ass. It had been stupid, him getting caught in the first place. He hadn't even been hunting Pettigrew. After he'd caught sight of Joe Small in Abilene, he'd tracked the sonofabitch into hell's country where rattlers were the closest thing to friendly that a man saw.

But Joe had seemed to know where he was going and instead of capturing him when he could have, Deacon got curious—and careless. He'd followed his outlaw quarry through a series of interconnecting canyons, not realizing that sentries aimed rifles down at him from the rim above. He'd been destined to die as soon as he'd entered the stone maze.

"I never told you thank you." He shuddered, remembering. He'd been praying for a quick death when she'd saved him.

"You can do that now." She began to explore, caressing his shaft, tracing a vein to the head of his cock, swirling her finger over his slit before curling her palm around his thickness. He covered her hand with his, guiding it up and down, his hips rising from the water thrusting more of his dick in her hand as she tightened her grip and pumped him.

She leaned over his shoulder and he thought she was admiring his cock. He was startled when she laid a trail of kisses from behind his ear to the spot where his neck met his shoulder then lower, brushing her lips across his scars. He groaned when she licked him there.

It was all he could handle. If he didn't get out of the water and in bed in a moment he'd have her spread in the tub, pounding into her.

"What should I call you, sweetheart?" he asked gruffly as he stood, lifting her with him, her legs still wrapped around his torso.

"Sweetheart's fine," she said, clinging to his back and laughing out loud.

Deacon laughed too. His fully aroused, rock-hard cock pointed at the bed as a beautiful woman rode him piggy back, her legs wrapping his waist and her heated core rubbing his back. The joy of being alive unfurled inside him.

Her giggles stopped after he crossed the room. She unlocked her legs and slid from his back to stand beside him, facing the bed. He turned, gazing over her long limbs and strong beauty.

She trembled when he let his hand travel down the curve of her waist, stopping to caress her flat belly before dropping lower. Her nether curls, the same blonde color adorning her head, formed a pale triangle between her thighs.

"Spread your legs." He ran his finger down the lips of her sex, holding her gaze as she loosened her thighs. Stroking the soft folds of flesh, he coaxed her until honey flowed from her channel and she relaxed her rigid stance.

Deacon played in her liquid heat before sliding his finger inside her. She flinched at his touch and her channel clenched as if it sought to repel the intruder. He pulled out and coated his digit with her slippery essence before testing her size again. This time he pulled her closer, pressing her body against his as his finger circled her entrance, teasing her sensitive flesh until she relaxed and moaned.

The wind kicked up, howling in the night outside, and she shivered against him, chill bumps racing over her flesh. He reached behind her and grabbed the cover from the bed, pulling it around her shoulders.

"Thank you. I'm not partial to cold," she explained.

"I'll keep you warm," he promised, loving the soft cadence of her speech.

Deacon laid her on the sheet, covering her body with his before inserting his leg between hers and spreading her thighs. He drew his knee higher until it brushed her lower curls.

"Still cold?" He held himself above her, his chest touching her breasts, his face close enough to hers for his murmured question to brush her lips.

Her head jerked sideways indicating *no*. He couldn't wait any longer and nudged her legs wider. Aligning his cock with her channel, he imagined plunging through her tight passage. But she wasn't ready. He rubbed the end of his shaft in her honey, wetting his cock before sliding it along her entrance instead of thrusting to her core as he wanted.

She tensed, squeezing her internal muscles so hard the end of his dick throbbed, threatening to spill. He stopped, staring down at her. She had her eyes screwed shut and her lower lip caught between her teeth.

"It's not supposed to be an unpleasant experience," he observed wryly.

"Sorry." She blinked at him owlishly. "Might take a time or two before I know what's what with you."

He stared into her eyes, feeling a tug of awareness at her words. But then the moment of uneasy recognition passed as he focused on the now. Her pupils were huge black dots obliterating the gray of the surrounding iris. Her skin was blanched of color and her breath came in shallow pants.

"Do you want me to stand down?" Though he offered, it was the last thing Deacon wanted to do.

"No," she gasped and threw a leg over his hip as if to hold him in place.

Deacon hadn't kissed a woman in over ten years—since his wife had died to be exact. He'd bedded females to ease his lust, spoken to them pleasantly when conversation demanded, even set up a short-term liaison once, testing the idea of maintaining a mistress. But kissing required a degree of intimacy he'd refrained from.

That changed when he gazed at the woman beneath him. Her mouth trembled as he nudged his cock through the opening to her channel.

"Relax, sweetheart," he murmured. His breath mingled with hers as they stared into each other's eyes. And then he took possession of her lips, slid his hand under her rump to tilt her to a better angle and swallowed her cry of surprise as he thrust inside.

He couldn't stop. An animallike roar gathered inside him as he penetrated her sheath, tearing through the barrier that had guarded her innocence.

It was hard to say who was more shocked in that moment—Deacon or the virgin prostitute who'd just been deflowered.

"I'm your first." He grunted in disbelief, staring into teary eyes that were also crinkled in mirth.

"You might be my last too, if it's all like this." She giggled, surprising him with her flash of humor.

He wanted to ask her why in hell she was whoring in a brothel for Lydia Lynch, but set aside such questions for later. For the moment, he concentrated on pleasing her and making this a night to always remember.

"Can't be responsible for making your first time a bad time," he assured her. He began to move, stretching her passage with slow, easy thrusts, straining to hold himself above her and show her the tenderness a woman's first time deserved.

When he bent to take her mouth again, she opened her lips to him, threading her fingers through his hair and stroking the back of his head as he deepened the kiss. His cock filled her below and his tongue above.

But he could feel the difference in her. She followed his moves stiffly, unsure. Sweat dripped from him and pooled between her breasts. He ducked his head and sucked on first one nipple, then the other. When he bit the tip, she gasped and clutched his head, holding his mouth against her flesh.

"Deacon," she moaned, dropping her legs from his waist as she arched her back, grinding her tender flesh against his groin, squeezing the walls of her channel around his rod.

It was too much pleasure and sent him into a frenzied release. He thrust and thrust, barely withdrawing in time to rear back and splatter his seed on her belly instead of in her womb.

He grabbed the washcloth he'd laid next to the bed and wiped his ejaculate from her flesh, then cleaned streaks of virgin blood from her thighs before dragging the bedcovers over them. Matching his length to hers, he pulled her into his embrace and collapsed. He felt almost belligerent beneath the satiated glow of completion. He'd just bedded a virgin. A maidenhead, whether it was given in a bawdy house or a marriage bed, was never to be disdained.

"Thank you for the gift of your innocence," he murmured gruffly when the sound of her breathing calmed.

"Well, if we're thankin' each other, much obliged for the..." She searched for a word and even her voice seemed to change as she continued. "Thank you very much for the lovely experience."

Her formal response brushed aside Deacon's ripple of almost recognition. He dropped his hand to stroke the soft curls on her mound and she winced. He sighed. Greed wasn't a good thing and he'd already had much more than he'd expected.

"You're too tender for more of my attentions. Right now I want to hold you in my arms. Food will be delivered soon. Rest with me until it arrives. Then we'll talk, all right?"

He settled his lips against her soft nape, breathing in her scent before trailing kisses down to the supple join of shoulder and neck. Deacon pressed one hand against her belly and the other cupped her breast as he fitted his chest to her back.

"Your fur tickles," she whispered and laughed softly.

He loosened his grip and put inches between them.

Just like that, she flipped around in his arms and leaned against him, rubbing her cheek against his chest hair, then fitting their body parts together as if they'd always slept in each other's arms. She matched her length against his, letting her nipples caress his chest, her leg slide between his thighs and her arms wrap around his neck.

"Much better," she whispered.

I'll take her with me when I leave in the morning. He made his plans as he held her and drifted in satiated pleasure. He didn't know exactly yet what he'd do with her, but her future wasn't going to be spent whoring for Lydia Lynch in Hell's Half Acre.

"I'm just damned glad it was me you drew as your first customer, sweetheart," he murmured against her hair. Closing his eyes, he matched his breathing to hers, trying to convince his mammoth erection it was time to rest.

Sublime torture was interrupted by a knock on the door. At the same moment, the clock chimed midnight.

"Dinner's served," he muttered.

Chapter Two

Miri watched with interest as Deacon pulled on a pair of clean pants and crossed to the door. She'd always found his size attractive.

"You've lost weight during your illness," she remarked as he rolled the serving cart toward the bed.

"Better skinny than dead," Deacon answered.

Miri retrieved the shirt she'd been wearing, making a moue of distaste at its damp, wrinkled state.

"Wear one of mine," Deacon suggested. After he parked the cart next to the small dining table in the room, he tossed her a shirt from his saddlebags.

It was better quality than what she usually wore. She didn't have to inspect it to know that Deacon's shirt was custom made. The finished seams caressing her flesh confirmed the superiority. That in turn reminded her that he was an educated man she didn't want to appear a fool in front of. *Keep your lips sealed and you'll be fine.*

Her audacity at being in this room with Deacon McCallister left her speechless. After a year of wistfully staring at her rival from afar, she'd done it — tasted forbidden fruit.

Miri had hung around Eclipse long enough to ascertain McCallister was on the road to recovery before returning to the task of tracking the spread of phony money through Texas and the Territory. It was the biggest case she'd ever pursued and she was determined to catch the criminals involved. She'd gathered what information Hiram had about the three men spreading fake money and followed his leads to other towns where bills had been found.

Finally she'd narrowed her pursuit to one man, a Texas cowboy named Ned Jackson, but Jackson's trail had frequently crossed the other two men's, Collier Syms, an Eastern banker, and Jefferson Landau, a Southern preacher. Being adept at disguises herself, she figured out fast that Syms, Landau and Jackson were all the same man.

She'd found the pretend minister real soon but instead of catching him, she'd decided to watch Landau, hoping he'd lead her to the plates he'd used to print his phony money. She followed him to Dodge and attended a tent service that started before the dew on the ground was dry.

Landau was preaching and the tent was jammed with saved sinners. He probably wouldn't have gotten more than the usual two bits but he salted the mine, so to speak. Every once in a while, a churchgoer waving a hundred dollar bill would jump up and praise Jesus. The lucky men and women claimed they'd found money after giving.

"Proverb 21:26," Landau had shouted. "The righteous give without sparing." He'd started his service in the morning and by afternoon, lines had formed outside with folks waving dollars and trying to get in the tent to put money in the collection plate and praise God.

She knew there was no mistake and Landau was her crook. Figuring that finding the plates would pay a bigger reward, Miri had held off taking him prisoner, hoping he'd lead her to the source of the bills.

He'd gotten away and it had taken her two more weeks to find another clue. This time she'd found Jackson. After studying the information that had been gathered by lawmen and comparing it to hers, she could see that whether there were three or one, two of the identities had something in common. One time or another, Syms and Landau had both visited the Pleasure Dome in Fort Worth. She'd based her next move on her conviction that Ned Jackson would show up at the brothel. The same day she quit looking in Wichita Falls, she traveled to Fort Worth.

When she'd arrived she could see that the section of town called Hell's Half Acre had sprawled way past its allotted size. She didn't much care for the wild goings-on but didn't figure to stay in the city of sin any longer than it took to complete the task at hand.

She was on the hunt when she'd struck up an acquaintance with Mrs. Lydia Lynch, the owner of the house of ill repute named the Pleasure Dome. The brothel owner needed a new butler and Miri needed to get inside the fancy whorehouse. Her path to success seemed destined to include butlering. Getting hired wasn't as easy as it sounded though.

The first time Miri applied for the job, she'd been wearing her Beau Beauregard clothes. She'd climbed a great number of fancy steps to a door decorated in gold and painted blue. When she knocked, the man who opened up was a bruiser. He took one look at her and said, "Sales, produce and complaints, take 'em around back."

Before he could get the door shut, Miri had explained in Beau's Tennessee drawl that she wasn't in trade and she wanted to apply for the butler's job. Miri could see why Lydia needed a new butler. The temporary doorman laughed out loud and shut the door in her face.

Not one to give up easily, Miri had made the trip to the back door, memorizing the hidey-holes of the guards stationed along the way. When she'd presented Beau this time, she'd received a sympathetic look from a kitchen worker along with a suggestion.

"Don't bother applying. Lydia only hires pretty boys to do her butlering."

Wearing shaggy brown hair topped by a floppy hat, Beau was country for sure. The young bounty hunter always made a point of drawling and smoking and keeping Miri's face mostly concealed so that folks remembered the thick accent instead of more telling features like her eyes.

Having a wolf trot beside her probably had a lot to do with leaving an impression too. In that light, it had been easy to see that her Beau disguise wasn't the right fit for Lydia's doorman. Grumbling at the expense, she'd visited Osgood's Theatrical Supplies and invested in a suit and a new hairpiece.

Already having spent more than she wanted, she'd shaved costs by renting a stall for Possum in the town livery, then sleeping in it too. In her opinion, with Ketchum sprawled outside the stall on guard, she was about the safest person in Hell's Half Acre.

The next morning Miri had knocked on the door as Calvin, a young gentleman wearing a vest, black frock coat, a gold pocket watch, dark sideburns and neatly trimmed hair. This time she'd been ushered to the brothel owner's office, where she was subjected to her first fondling.

"No padding at all," Lydia had purred, feeling Miri's shoulders and admiring the way the coattails hung in the back. "Calvin, you'll do."

Lydia had explained that her place was high class and her employee at the entrance had to dress accordingly. She'd been more concerned with appearance then protection. She'd introduced Miri to two of the men she employed to handle what she called *incidents* and made it clear that Calvin was only expected to be polite and answer the door.

And just look who Calvin invited in. Miri buttoned Deacon's shirt, loving the subtle smell of tobacco and soap clinging to it. *If he has one of his cigars after dinner I'll beg for a puff.* She watched, mesmerized, as Deacon peeled the white cover from the suite's table to reveal a setting for two. Deftly he turned the wineglasses upright, filled each one with sparkling brew and handed her a glass.

It probably isn't much different than beer. She hesitated.

He picked up a strawberry and swirled it in the liquid, then held it to her lips.

"Oh." The flavor burst over her tongue as she sank her teeth into the juicy fruit.

She nibbled her way to the green stem then licked his fingers, gratified to hear him stifle a groan.

He deftly unbuttoned her shirt and brushed the sides apart, displaying her breasts. Heat coiled in her belly, anticipating what he might do next. He swirled another strawberry in the wine, then rubbed it over her nipple before licking the drops of liquid from her now turgid peak.

His engorged shaft pushed against loosely buttoned pants. Before she could change her mind, she reached down and freed his hard length. As he suckled her breast, she pushed him down on one of the armless dining room chairs, straddling him and sinking down on his cock.

Miri cupped her breasts so that he might better suckle while he gripped her hips and set the tempo of their ride.

"Tender?" he asked her as she tightened the walls of her channel around his hard length.

"Hurts good." She told him the truth and that seemed to free some restraint he'd been under. He nipped her breast then applied suction to the tip, sending hot bolts of lust radiating from her nipple to her sex.

She spread her thighs and flexed her knees, raising and lowering herself on his shaft, each thrust allowing deeper penetration until his cock head lodged against her core.

Oh my, yes. She closed her eyes. She'd waited a long time to try this out and planned to take full advantage of the opportunity since it was doubtful she'd ever get another chance to bed him. He cupped her breasts, kneading them and pressing his thumbs against her nipples as he took her mouth in a kiss.

She'd never tongue-kissed anyone before Deacon tonight. While she tried to get the hang of doing it, he stroked the nubbin of nerves at the top of her cleft, thrusting his hips up and sinking deeper inside of her at the same time. She followed his rhythm and it was what Miri imagined dancing must be like.

Her sex fisted around Deacon's cock and her channel squeezed him as her back arched against the tension. Pulling her mouth from his, she gasped in panicked protest.

"Deacon…" she managed to get out before ecstasy pulsed in her womb. Her hips moved, chasing bliss.

"Don't stop, sweetheart," he growled. He stiffened, tried to stand, sat back down and grabbed her rump, grinding his pelvis into the lips of her sex and sealing them together. She felt the hot pulse of his seed against the walls of her channel.

It was amazing and scary and not at all like the first time they'd coupled, which had been interesting. This time she was embarrassed, lethargic with pleasure and left feeling vulnerable. She'd clearly misplaced her mind.

"I lost control," he muttered.

Well, all right. He'd lost his head too. She blinked, not realizing until that moment her eyes had been shut tight and she was biting her lip. Her gaze locked with his. He looked stern, forbidding. She still had his cock inside of her. It was awkward.

"I sure am hungry." Not knowing what else to say, she eased off him, dropped a napkin over his lap and grabbed his shirt. Retreating to a spot behind the fancy screen, she cleaned herself, again feeling that flush of intense awareness of her body, him and what they'd done.

As she washed away their mingled emissions she tried to get a grip on her emotions. It had been a momentary aberration. A loss of good sense. Now she'd have to deal with possible repercussions from her insane behavior.

She tidied herself, pulling on his shirt. He was bare-chested, wearing only pants when she returned to the table. He stood, seating her on the chair as if she were a lady before he dropped a kiss on her head and began filling a plate from the different selections on the serving cart. When he handed it to her, she avoided his gaze.

"Hope this is pheasant." Lydia's chef was famous. Miri had sampled a few bites on her way through the kitchen during the last week and knew it was food like she'd never had before. Flustered by her own feelings, she concentrated on the meal and not the man across the table.

When she heard the clink of cutlery against china, she risked a peek at him. He'd filled his plate and ate with gusto. She returned to her food, adjusting the way she held her fork to match his.

Everything was moving along well until he began to question her. She should have known that Deacon McCallister was incapable of setting aside work for pleasure.

"How do you know Lydia?"

"What difference does it make?" she mumbled, forgetting to use the seductive voice she'd assigned this role.

"How long have you been here at the Pleasure Dome? Did Beauregard send you in to scout for him?" He prodded her for more information.

"Why?" Miri laid her fork down and stared across the table at him. His inquisition ruined the moment and she set aside the impulse to bury her face against his chest and rub her nose in his scent.

He stood, placing his napkin carefully on his chair. She noted the gesture in case she had an occasion for fine dining in the future, which was doubtful.

"You were a virgin," he repeated as if that had some significance she'd overlooked.

"Was. Not anymore."

"I don't bed virgins," he declared.

"Too late," she answered and took the last strawberry from the dish to nibble while he said what he had to say.

"When I next see Beauregard, I'm going to kick his ass from here to Sunday. This is the second time the toad-eater has sent you into danger. You will leave this den of iniquity with me in the morning. Dammit, this has got to stop. Do you understand?"

"Yes." She bit down on the strawberry, wishing the flood of sweet juice would erase the bitter taste of regret in her mouth.

"Fine. Come to bed. We'll sleep and then sort things out tomorrow." His tone lost its autocratic menace and a half-smile curved his lips. He moved her back to the bed and took charge. And she let him. He was tender, rough, giving, demanding and everything Miri had ever imagined he'd be.

"Feel good?" he whispered in her ear as he cupped her mound, parting her folds and playing in her wet heat.

Good doesn't do it justice. Sliding her long mane to one side, she exposed her neck to his lips. She was greedy for sensation. "Don't be gentle," she ordered him.

New though she was at this, Miri reached behind her and clasped his cock, guiding it toward her entrance. She felt him shudder and groan as she fisted her hand around him and pumped his hard length. He brought her to her knees, pressed her shoulders to the mattress and lifted her hips.

She wasn't quite sure what came next. For a moment she felt like a fool with her bottom waving in the air and her sexual center exposed.

But when he teased her, rubbing his shaft against the tender flesh inside the lips of her sex, she moaned her approval. Then he brushed the end of his cock against her pearl, making it pulse with need. She was embarrassed at the amount of liquid emissions her body produced. "I'm dripping. Maybe you should dry—" He thrust.

Miri turned her face into the mattress and screamed. When Deacon froze she whispered fiercely. "That was a good sound not a bad. I'm a big girl and I won't break. I want this. Don't stop."

From that point on, he didn't. Miri swayed with each thrust. His cock was hot and hard, pushing its way through folds of flesh that clenched, trying to hold on.

She arched her back and shifted her thighs wider, taking as much of him as she could. Each time he slid in, he seemed to penetrate deeper than the time before.

"Want more?" He thrust, pulled back and thrust again.

"Yes," she panted. "Yes, yes, yes."

"What about this?" He pulled her up and back on his lap, seating himself so deep her buttocks splayed open. Before she caught her breath, he cupped both breasts, took the nipples between his fingers and pinched.

Miri's knees were tucked under her on either side of his hips. She ground her sex against his groin, letting him know this time she was in charge. He growled incoherent words of delight. She angled her head as he nipped down the line of her jaw, finally turning her head completely for his kiss.

His tongue breached her lips and she forgot everything but bliss as she lifted, came down on his cock and then rose again.

"You like that?" He stroked the nubbin of nerves at the apex of her sex, making her womb clench and milk his hard length as spasms of pleasure rippled through her.

"That's mighty fine," she gasped.

He ran his fingers through her wetness, stroking the soft inner lining of her cleft as he used his other hand to toy with her nipples.

"You're new at this and I'm a greedy swine. Let me just hold you the rest of the night." He offered to stop.

Miri wasn't having any of that. He was hers for the night and she planned on enjoying him as long as she could.

It had been early evening when she'd entered the room. It was early morning when they lay in a tangle of body parts, replete and exhausted.

"Dammit," Deacon cursed quietly. "Back itches," he muttered. He sat up and scooted higher on the mattress, scratching the newly healed flesh on his back against the headboard.

Miri rolled him over so that Deacon sprawled on his front. She trailed her fingers up and down his back, rubbing more than scratching.

He groaned his thanks and practically purred under her attentions. Finally, he pulled her down beside him and arranged her so she was anchored to the bed by his arm.

"Sleep, sweetheart," he ordered her, dropping a kiss on her forehead before he took his own advice and snored.

The way Deacon treats a woman is sure different from the way he treats a man. Miri lay in Deacon's arms, savoring the sound of his exhaustion as she tried to keep herself awake

I've known him for over a year — spying on him, deviling him, dogging him — and finally saving his dadblamed butt. Reckon this wasn't a hasty coupling. Miri patted his rump possessively and grinned as she mentally catalogued what she'd learned, aside from her carnal education, which she'd think about later.

Napkin goes on chair when finished dining, man pulls out lady's chair, champagne fizzes, pheasant tastes like chicken. As her body cooled, unexpected aches replaced points of satisfaction and she repressed more than one groan. Carefully, she freed herself from Deacon's embrace, edging toward the side of the bed. She couldn't resist one last look at him and reared up on her arm to peer through the half light at his body.

He was something, all right. She grinned, enjoying the sight of his muscled shoulders and strong thighs. She considered licking a drop of sweat to memorize his flavor, though she'd already sampled his taste earlier.

He shifted from his front to his back and as she watched, the weight of sleep settled over him and his snores deepened. She grinned wickedly, wishing she could tease him about the sounds he made when he slept.

Miri closed her eyes, distinguishing his male scent from the heady perfume left from their intimacy. One last time, she inhaled deeply, holding the essence of Deacon McCallister in her lungs before she sighed, released her breath and reluctantly focused.

Game over. Her pursuit of a criminal had certainly taken her to an unexpected location this time. Hell's Half-Acre wasn't a town she'd usually favor, but it had led her into Deacon McCallister's arms—a place she'd only dreamed about.

She smacked herself mentally. *Get up!* If she didn't retrieve her prisoner soon, she was going to have a lot of explaining to do when he turned up dead under the back porch. Panic filled her and she mentally batted it away.

A lamp across the room glowed, softly outlining the way of escape. The key to the room lay on the same dresser where Miri had hastily stuffed Calvin's suit. Sanity urged her to get up and get out.

As if sensing that she intended to leave, Deacon shifted, pulling her into his embrace and eliminating the inches she'd gained as she'd crept toward the edge of the mattress. Lord, he was warm. His chest radiated heat against her back. She resisted temptation, staying awake by recounting the steps she'd taken to get herself in this position. As of yesterday morning, she'd been on the job more than a week and as expected, she'd had no trouble with the men coming and going.

Her boss though, had been another matter. Lydia had a penchant for finding excuses to touch her butler. Had it not been so important to keep the job, Miri would have quit, but as it was, she'd tied flat her bosom, making certain there wasn't a thing for Lydia to feel but the very real muscle's in Miri's arms when she was running her hands up and down the suit jacket.

Since she'd been hired as Calvin, she'd avoided Lydia's endless tweaks, pats and outright groping by staying out of her sight. The owner of the Pleasure Dome was a busy woman and it didn't take more than one session with Lydia for Miri to memorize the madam's schedule and hope Jackson appeared before Miri gave up and quit being Calvin the butler.

Two nights before, her whole bounty hunting scheme had flirted with disaster. Adam Crispin, the owner of a card hell down the street, had spent the evening upstairs. Lydia had walked with him down the steps as if they'd been together. She'd stood watching as he departed, making certain that he was actually going.

Miri used her formal attire and manner to sustain her role as the gentleman butler. She exhibited a half bow when admitting clients and a tilt of the head when she bade them good night. It had worked and she'd had no problem remaining anonymous and ignored. However, when Miri inclined her head at Crispin, he lunged and tried to grab Calvin's cods.

Miri had been opening the door for the bastard when suddenly he had her pinned against it, sliding his hand down her front toward her privates. She'd caught his wrist before the grope was completed and grabbed his crotch instead. He was shorter than her by a head and she had no trouble subduing him.

Squeezing his very real balls, she'd more or less lifted him by his shoulder and half dragged, half backed him to the sidewalk. Once there, she'd made a show of picking him up and tossing him into the street.

When he'd landed, he'd gone for the fancy gun he kept hidden. She'd been expecting it. Since her new suit jacket came complete with some interesting pouches and inner pockets, she'd already palmed her knife, ready to throw. She'd pinned his sleeve to the ground before he could get off a shot.

Two Pleasure Dome bouncers had taken charge and convinced the customer to leave quietly. It could have gone differently. It hadn't. But it had drawn Lydia's attention.

Miri had spent the rest of the night in front of the Pleasure Dome using her cigarettes as an excuse to remain there. Lydia didn't take to smoking, and any employee who entertained the vice had to do so outside. Miri's defection from inside door duty went unchallenged. Any customers who arrived, she escorted to the front door, opened it and saw them in before returning to the street below.

Both of Lydia's guards on outside night patrol had made it a point to compliment her handling of Adam Crispin. Carl, the older of the two, had offered advice.

"Calvin, you'll get pulled into a lot of not nice things here. You seem like a decent sort, which means you aren't for this place. 'Twas it me, I'd be moving on before Lydia moved me up."

"I've been meaning to ask. What happened to the last butler?"

"Crispin." Carl spat on the ground.

At dawn, the night watch went inside to eat breakfast, leaving the courtyard around the Pleasure Dome unguarded but for her. It was a mark of respect from Lydia's guards that they trusted Calvin to stand watch while they were inside.

Miri had been standing on the walk, considering the possibility of leaving and not returning. Fate in the guise of Ned Jackson, or whatever he was calling himself these days, intervened. Ned rode down Rusk Street on a fancy bay, stopped in front of the Pleasure Dome, climbed down and handed her his reins.

"Take care of my animal and there's a sawbuck in it for you." While he'd fished in his pocket for a bill, she'd stepped close enough to take the reins and press her derringer against his side.

"If it's a tenner you printed yourself, no thanks," she'd drawled. "Walk with me, Ned. I've something to show you."

Miri had found that most people responded to the calm voice of reason. Leading the horse and discreetly jamming her gun in Ned's ribs, she'd reasoned him all the way to the back, intending to go to the barn, fetch Possum and leave.

She was closer to the house than the barn when a light went on in the kitchen. Before Ned could squawk or make a fuss, she'd bashed him on the skull, gagged him, tied him and rolled his body under the porch. Then she'd had a spare horse to explain, so she'd led the beast to the barn and stabled it.

She was almost to the porch with Possum, intending to hoist Ned over the saddle and leave before the day guards arrived when one of Lydia's inside guards, Benjamin, had stepped outside.

"Lydia wants to speak to you."

"I'm done for the day." She'd tried to fob him off, pointing at Possum.

"Not until you've talked to the boss." He'd stood holding the door open for her expectantly. She'd tied Possum to a hitching post and like a lamb to the slaughter she'd gone back into the Pleasure Dome, hoping to avoid another pawing from the madam.

Lydia had been waiting in the hall and as soon as Miri walked through the back entrance, the madam's hand had been on her butler's arm, her fingers lingering a little longer than necessary.

"A knife, Calvin? You continually surprise me." She'd felt up Miri's suit sleeve, this time looking for more than muscle. "Crispin was only admiring my handsome butler. I'm sure he meant no harm." She'd patted Miri's arm playfully but her tone had been sharp.

"If you want to get rich quick, Calvin, there's plenty besides that awkward sod who'd pay good money for what's inside these clothes."

"No ma'am. Just interested in downstairs work." She'd removed the hand fondling her arm.

Miri stood at least a half a foot taller than the petite madam and no doubt outweighed her by fifty pounds. The wig Calvin wore was one of the best theatrical props sold and it wouldn't come off unless she wanted it to. But it wasn't fear of Lydia discovering her gender that had alarmed Miri. The madam's cold appraisal had given Miri chills.

"In the future, use your good sense, Calvin. Such public evictions give a place a bad name." Then she'd given a throaty laugh. "I have to admit, the way you booted that nincompoop out was precious. I loved it when you had him by the nuts, walking him backward down the steps."

Miri had been all set to leave. Possum was tied out back, ready to go. The job was finished. She'd captured her quarry and outmaneuvered her employer's rule of sanctuary.

It was a sorry truth that Lydia's brothel was considered neutral territory. The law was well paid to leave the customers alone until they departed the premises. To Miri's way of thinking, men had a funny way of conducting business. They might consider the brothel a safe house for all—but she didn't.

She'd caught her counterfeiter, he was going to justice and she was hauling his bones there. Unless he squawked about where he'd been caught, no one would know. If they found out, she'd swear to the truth—Ned Jackson had been on Rusk Street not inside the grounds of the Pleasure Dome when she'd taken him prisoner.

Success still waited under the back steps. Ned was worth fifteen hundred dollars as soon as she delivered him to the Fort Worth sheriff's jail.

But here she lay in the bed next to Deacon, recounting the many ways her plan had gone right at the same time it had been skidding awry. After her talk with Lydia had interrupted her extraction of Jackson there had been too many tradesmen coming and going in the morning to return to him. So she'd left Possum saddled and ready while she continued to play doorman and waited for a chance to remove Ned discreetly from under the porch.

When the morning rush had calmed, she'd been ready to head for the back of the house. She'd worked all night. No one would have faulted Calvin had the butler let Lydia's security detail answer the knock at the front door.

But she hadn't and fate had intervened again. She'd opened it to confront her nemesis — rival bounty hunter Deacon McCallister — and the man she'd been ogling and sighing over for better than a year. At that point, things all went to hell.

Thank God, Deacon had barely glanced at the Pleasure Dome butler. But then again, had he done so, Miri assured herself, it wouldn't have mattered. It had been bounty hunter Beau Beauregard Deacon had exchanged insults with, not a harmless doorman named Calvin. Nevertheless, she'd hurried him to Lydia's fancy sitting room intending to retrieve her prisoner and leave fast.

So why was she in bed with Deacon McCallister, grinning like a loon? It was a fact that she'd always had a hankering for him. She reined in her exuberance and concentrated on getting on with the job of collecting her prisoner and taking him to jail.

Had she not been hanging around outside the sitting room door eavesdropping, she probably could have made her escape with Ned in hand then. But she'd heard Deacon discuss counterfeit money with Lydia and had lingered. From that point on, she'd altered her plan moment by moment, risking her prize in order to be here.

When Lydia had almost caught her lurking outside the door, Miri had squeezed hurriedly into the broom closet on the first floor. From there, she'd heard the madam send the new girl, Melanie, up to wait in Deacon's room.

As soon as the way was clear, Miri reemerged as Calvin and hastened behind the girl, redirecting her to another room. It had been simple then to slide into Deacon's suite and wait for him. She hadn't any fancy nightwear, so she'd settled for her butler shirt to cover the parts of her that needed covering.

She'd have liked to stay until morning, though that risk was unjustifiable. Anyway, no matter if she wanted to cuddle in Deacon's arms and have one more bout of loving to remember the rest of her life—she couldn't. For the sake of her prisoner, she had to leave. And it was just as well.

Deacon was all set to kick up a ruckus in the morning and she didn't think it would be a good idea to hang around for the event. Besides, cool and dark under the porch though it was, Ned Jackson was probably a mite thirsty by now. He'd been quiet, but that didn't surprise Miri either.

She'd left Ketchum guarding him and the wolf she hunted with would keep Ned silent. Carefully, Miri shifted toward the edge of the bed, putting real distance between her and Deacon as he rolled on his side, dropping his arm to clutch a pillow.

It was all she needed to slip from under the covers and make a beeline for the dresser where he'd left the key to the door. She pulled her wig and butler suit from their hiding place in the drawer and slid into the pants, retrieving the white shirt from the floor and tucking her shirttails in.

She picked up the pearl button he'd cut from the shirt and Miri cast a quick look at the bed. Deacon was on his side facing the opposite wall. Quickly she hid her hair under the wig, unlocked the door and stepped into the hall before again turning the key in the lock and sliding it under the door for him to find in the morning.

Though it was the predawn hour when few were stirring and the house was at its quietest, it took all of her skill to avoid running into Lydia Lynch's security detail prowling the hallways. She passed through the kitchen where one of the outside guards stood drinking a cup of coffee and talking to the chef. Miri knew it was time to make her move.

Dawn was turning the night sky pink when she crawled under the porch and pulled Jackson from underneath the steps by the scruff of his neck. After a day laying in his own sweat and piss, he was a smell to be reckoned with. One whiff and she had to clench her teeth to keep from retching.

She ripped his gag off and handed him a canteen for a drink. When she started to slap the gag back on, he thrashed around and fought her until Ketchum got in his face and growled. Having a wolf assist in captures convinced a lot of the outlaws to cooperate.

With Ketchum by his side and Miri's gun against his back, Jackson was docile. She walked him to her mount and once there, didn't give him time to fuss or fight. Shoving her shoulder into his gut, she lifted Ned and laid him belly-down over Possum's saddle. Ketchum stood guard as Miri stepped in the shadows to transform herself.

She made quick work of donning Beau's heavy buckskins, pulling on the bounty hunter clothes in a bulky layer on top of the butler's suit. They were welcome since the weather had turned cold. She removed the leather spats from her feet and transferred the fancy shoes to her saddle bag.

It was doubtful she'd again find use for them, but she'd keep them in case she needed them in another disguise. She removed Calvin's short wig, kept her own hair pinned high, pulled on Beau's wig of light brown hair cut in a ragged style, and slapped on her floppy hat. Once she'd laced up her knee-high moccasins and pulled on her duster it was Beau Beauregard riding his pinto and carrying outlaw cargo down Rusk Street.

Before the sun had completely reached above the horizon, the young bounty hunter had delivered

Ned to jail and collected a promissory note. The release for the reward would be wired to the Eclipse Bank as soon as the U.S. marshal certified that the prisoner in jail was the same man on the poster.

When the payment was released, Beau Beauregard, a bounty hunter well known in Eclipse, would withdraw the funds and Miri would be set for winter. That's when she'd relax, put on the shirt of Deacon's she'd worn and subsequently purloined. That's when she'd let herself remember.

Chapter Three

Deacon was already awake and getting dressed when the key turned in the hotel lock. In pants only, holding his gun in hand, he faced the door, greeting the Pleasure Dome goons when they entered his room. Lydia was not far behind.

"Where is he?" she demanded.

"Who?" There was no one in the bed with him. But the scent of sex and tangled sheets testified that he hadn't been lonely during the night.

"Don't play innocent," Lydia said coldly. "I have a steady customer who enjoys the safety of the Pleasure Dome when he's in town. His horse is in the stable but he's not in the house."

"He's not in here either." Deacon shrugged and pulled a clean shirt from his saddlebag. "And I wasn't bounty hunting last night."

"Was Calvin in here?"

"Excuse me?" That gave him pause. Why the hell would Lydia think her butler had visited him? She answered before he asked.

"My butler as well as my customer is missing. Melanie says she was on her way to your room yesterday afternoon when Calvin rerouted her to another room." Lydia looked with interest at the wrinkled sheets. "You obviously didn't spend the night alone."

Deacon didn't argue about Calvin or try to convince Lydia that her butler hadn't visited his room. Nor did he disclose the real occupant of his bed the night before. The two security men in his suite remained by the madam's side, setting off alarm bells in Deacon's head.

They were bruisers who kept the brothel's working girls in line as much as the Pleasure Dome visitors. He concentrated on convincing Lydia he hadn't poached in her territory by nabbing one of her customers. She lost interest in him and left. Before the door was completely closed, she peeked around the edge.

"Robert, I had no idea you favored that persuasion."

Alone again, he searched the room, including flipping back the bed coverlet. His memory hadn't been false. He removed the bottom sheet, folded it and put it in his saddlebag, then left enough money on the nightstand to cover the cost of the expensive bedding.

He had no desire to discuss her with Lydia but he intended to talk to his companion from the night before. No butler was on duty when he descended the steps but Lydia appeared and walked beside him toward the door.

"I take it I'm not having breakfast," he said wryly.

"I'd prefer that you leave without a fuss," Lydia said when he stopped in the foyer.

"I'm not leaving without talking to the woman you sent to my room last night. She was as tall as most men, slender with a full bosom and had pale blonde hair falling long and straight."

"I don't know who you spent the night with. I'm sure my elusive butler Calvin could explain if we could find him. I think he was busy kidnapping one of my guests." Lydia glared at him, anger marring her usual serene composure. Deacon frowned back.

"I have no interest in the peculiarities of your doorman. He's well gone if he escaped your snare." He focused on Lydia and said grimly, "But I do care about the young woman who came to my room."

"If I knew who it was, I'd drag her here right now." When she continued to deny knowing the name of the girl, Deacon opened the front door and started down the steps.

It was obvious Lydia wanted something from him as she walked with him to the street below. When they reached the bottom tread, she laid her hand on his arm to stop him.

"Robert, I'm telling you the truth. Melanie is my tallest girl. If I can find the Amazon you've described, she'll be worth—"

Deacon's hand wrapped around Lydia's throat and he resisted the urge to throttle her. She gaped at him fearfully.

He dropped his hand, stepping away from the madam. The security guard aiming a gun at him was a chill reminder of the violence he'd almost unleashed.

He needed to find his night's companion. He had proof in his saddlebag that she'd not been a prostitute in her past. He intended to see to it she never was. The frustration of having no name and no way to find her again left him gritting his teeth.

His long strides carried him away from the Pleasure Dome and down the street toward the stable. It was a shock when Lydia's voice interrupted his thoughts as she hurried beside him, trying to keep up.

"Robert," she panted, urgently demanding his attention. She grabbed his arm, whether to secure his interest or keep from toppling over, Deacon wasn't sure. Since he'd choked the woman moments before, he stopped to see what was so important she braved his presence.

"I need you to go visit the Fort Worth sheriff's office and see if any prisoners were brought in this morning." White lines of tension showed around her mouth and her nails bit through the thickness of his shirt where she held on to him.

"Who am I asking about?"

"He goes by a lot of names." Lydia's answer spilled from her lips in a deluge of panic. "One of them is Ned Jackson. He was on his way here. He should have arrived yesterday. This morning, his horse is in my private barn but he's not in the house."

"And why should I care?" Deacon shrugged. He had no reason to help Lydia Lynch. On the other hand, here was Ned Jackson handed to him on a platter. He didn't bother telling her that her friend was a counterfeiter.

"You need to help me because Annie was my friend and she'd want you to do this for me." Lydia's voice took on the petulant sound of a young girl.

"I seriously doubt that, Lydia." But he had his own missing person to find. Since his quest began at the Pleasure Dome and he might need Lydia's help to find the mystery woman before it was done, he agreed to visit the law office.

"And if your friend is in jail and I get him out?"

"Bring him here."

* * * * *

Deacon's visit to the Fort Worth law office bore fruit. He had no trouble getting the sheriff to talk. The town merchants had protested his crackdown on crime in the area. It was cyclical. After enough murders took place and too many whores committed suicide, the merchants would want him to get busy again. Meanwhile, Harold Tully spent more time polishing his gun then using it.

"Yep, that youngster Beauregard hauled Ned in this morning. Said he was a counterfeiter and government agents would be interested in talking to him."

"You pay Beauregard?"

"I don't keep money here, Deacon. I gave the kid a promissory note. He can cash it at any bank as soon as the U.S. marshal comes in and confirms Ned is the man on the wanted poster."

Well damn. The mouthy brat, a constant point of irritation, had tracked Jackson to Fort Worth and caught him. Deacon admired the kid's skill at the same time he enjoyed putting a spoke in his wheel.

"You know he nabbed Jackson at Lydia's place? She's fit to be tied and sent me over here to see about it." As expected, Tully was so riled he was ready to slap Beauregard in jail and release Ned.

"No respect, Deacon. I'm telling you these young'uns coming up aren't like me and you. They've got no respect for the rules."

Deacon winced when the sheriff aligned their ages since Tully was sixty if he was a day and Deacon was thirty-three. Nevertheless, he let the image of old comrades fighting against insolent youth stand without comment.

Ned Jackson was duly brought out from the cell where he'd been sleeping. For having arrived only hours before, he looked pretty rough and smelled worse.

"You keeping pigs back there, Harold?" Deacon coughed and backed away from Jackson.

"Evidently, he rolled in his own filth for a while after the butler caught him." Harold wiped his eyes and then held a thick handkerchief over his nose.

"I thought you said Beau Beauregard brought him in."

"He did. But after Beauregard left, this one kept talking about the butler. He didn't make sense and smelled so bad I didn't spend a lot of time listening."

"I'm an innocent citizen." When it looked as if he was getting out based on the misdeeds of the bounty hunter, Ned offered a new version of the story and claimed he'd been attacked and dragged off the street by a crazy kid with a wolf.

Harold waved his hand at him, indicating he wanted him gone.

"Hope the Eclipse Bank doesn't jump the gun and pay that promissory note," Deacon drawled.

"I'll wire 'em soon as you leave," Harold assured him.

"I'll give your regards to Lydia." Deacon tipped his hat to Harold and followed Jackson out the door. As soon as the counterfeiter's foot hit the Fort Worth sidewalk, Deacon grabbed him from behind and nudged him toward the horse. "Lydia sent for you."

"Oh for God's sake. Your job's done. Turn me loose, you fool."

"Can't do it. I wouldn't want you to disappoint Lydia. That was a fine story you were telling inside. How about telling me now what really happened? Did the butler catch you or did Beauregard?"

"The squirrely bastards are one and the same. The butler was on the street when I arrived. He marched me behind the building, knocked me silly, tied me up like a Christmas turkey and shoved me under the porch."

Heat prickled under Deacon's skin, racing up to burn his face with a deep blush. He'd rather not have had Beauregard witness his visit to a whorehouse.

"What business did you have at Lydia's place?" Covering his discomposure, he questioned Ned.

"Same business every man has when he visits a whorehouse."

The brothel owner's outlaw friend wasn't forthcoming with more information and he needed a bath before Deacon was getting close enough to question him in depth. Until that happened, Deacon mounted his horse and walked behind Jackson, herding him down the street toward the Pleasure Dome.

Once there, Lydia smelled Ned and sent him to her private apartment to bathe. Deacon ordered breakfast and ate in the dining room. Clean and hungry, Ned wandered in with a plate stacked high with food.

"Still here, McCallister?" The counterfeiter was a banty rooster of a fellow and it seemed clear he wanted Deacon gone from Lydia's dining room. "You fetched for her. You can leave now."

He looked as if he had more to say but Lydia joined them for coffee. Ned suddenly had more interest in eating the crepes than talking to Lydia. She, on the other hand, demanded answers.

"You will tell me right now what you're involved in this time." Lydia demonstrated impatience rather than affection toward the outlaw.

"Siblings?" Deacon finished his coffee and set the cup down. His guess wasn't that outlandish since once he was cleaned up, Ned proved to be a masculine version of Lydia.

"Twins. I'm the respectable one," the notorious madam of the Pleasure Dome admitted grimly. "I've been trying to keep him out of jail all his life."

Ned didn't deny it and Deacon didn't doubt it. But he didn't waste sympathy on her. Ned's cutlery hit the plate as he finished his meal and Deacon laid his napkin on the table and stood.

"Ready to go, Ned?"

"Where?" brother and sister asked in unison.

"Eclipse, to jail. You were pretty ripe this morning. I just brought you here to clean up and grab breakfast before we hit the trail."

"No." Lydia wasn't having any of it. Ned didn't seem concerned at all about Deacon's intentions. In fact, before he hid his expression, he looked almost smug.

"I haven't been to Eclipse in years," he murmured lazily. "It will be just like old times visiting the MC3."

"When did you visit the ranch?" Deacon frowned, staring hard at Ned whose expression had become almost feral.

"Ned, let it go." Lydia groaned.

Ned shrugged and didn't let it go. "I visited Annie on the McCallister ranch to pay my respects after you married."

"I don't recall being introduced." Deacon stared at Lydia's twin. He'd never seen him before.

"That's because I didn't come to see you. I came to see her. Annie Ross was supposed to be my bride. I'd been away for a while. When I got back, you'd married my intended."

"You were gone and she changed her mind," Lydia defended her friend. "She wanted a respectable life, not the harum-scarum disorder you lived."

"She was mine long before you met her, McCallister." Ned's snarl was aimed at Deacon, implying that more than just a childhood friendship had existed between him and Annie.

Deacon considered Ned's claim. He sighed, resisting the urge to plant his fist in the other man's face. Deacon didn't think about those days often. But he remembered them. "Ned," he drawled, "if you visited Annie at the MC3, no wonder I didn't meet you. We didn't live there during our marriage. All in all, it sounds as if Annie was well rid of you."

"She loved me but married you and look where that got her." Ned ignored the fact that he'd been caught in his lie, continuing his attempt to needle Deacon.

"If you loved her so much, why didn't you settle down and marry her?" Deacon continued to let Ned bait him, but turned so that he faced both sister and brother. He couldn't be certain that their quarrel was even real.

"Because he was in jail," Lydia hissed.

"Then it will feel like home when he returns." Deacon slapped the cuffs on Ned and prepared to leave.

"That's not necessary," Ned protested.

"There's a wanted poster in the Fort Worth sheriff's office that says you're a counterfeiter and there are some government men who want to talk to you. Yep. The cuffs stay on."

"Counterfeiter?" Lydia screeched. "You swine. You've risked all I've built. I'm coming too."

"Lydia, I'm not hitching a buggy up for you and this isn't a pleasure trip into the country. Your twin's business is his business. Let it be." His wife had been a friend of Lydia's but as far as Deacon was concerned, Annie's reach didn't extend from the grave to protect Ned.

"Keep your mouth shut and maybe I'll be able to keep you out of jail this time too." Lydia glared at her brother. "I'll hire the bounty hunter who disguised himself as my butler."

"The one who shoved me under the porch and left me to die of thirst?" Ned was outraged.

"He fooled me and caught you. That means he's smart. I'll hire him to find the plates and the paper. The law will be so happy to have this business resolved, they'll thank me and forgive you."

Deacon didn't doubt that the madam would be able to keep her brother out of jail. One way and another she'd been manipulating men all of her life. Generals would have envied Lydia's ability to make plans in the midst of battle. She already had her scheme in place but that didn't change his.

"Suit yourself. But you're not traveling with us." Deacon considered both twins and knew without a doubt that Lydia was the more dangerous.

"Need some help, Lydia?" One of the bouncers in the shadowed area behind the stairs offered his assistance. She glanced his way and opened her mouth.

"If I have to fight my way out of here, I'll shoot your brother first and you second," Deacon murmured his warning before she could respond. He let his hand rest on his holster, ready to draw and fire if necessary. But as he'd hoped, Lydia did have affection for her brother and believed Deacon's threat.

"We're fine, Benjamin. Ned is leaving with Mr. McCallister."

Deacon ignored Lydia and her goon and jerked Ned out the door and to the barn. Nobody followed or attempted to stop them. He attached one end of Ned's cuff to an iron hitching ring while he saddled the animals and then gave Ned his choice.

"Cuffs stay on. You can ride in the saddle or across it. It makes no difference to me."

"Lock 'em in front so I keep my balance." Ned spoke agreeably.

"They'll stay locked behind. Fall off and you'll go across the saddle."

Deacon and Ned rode out of Fort Worth together. The prisoner's hands were cuffed behind his back and he wore a scowl on his face.

The better part of the morning was gone before either man broke the silence. Travel gave Deacon the time to mull over Ned's claim. He'd just learned that he'd been Annie's second choice. He'd courted her during the years he was at seminary and they'd developed a strong friendship. As though knowing where Deacon's thoughts lay, Ned decided to reminisce out loud.

"We were close as three peas in a pod growing up, Lydia, Annie and me. Sometimes Annie and me were closer than that. She lived on the ranch next to the played-out patch of ground our family squatted on."

Deacon remembered Annie's place with affection. There wasn't enough land to farm or ranch, but it had a nice view of the river. After they'd married, he and Annie had lived there for the six months before they moved to Abilene. He and his young bride had sat together on the porch steps thinking they'd have a lifetime together.

"Ned, it doesn't matter what did or didn't happen before Annie and I were wed." Deacon figured Ned was trying to provoke a fight, looking for a way out of his current fix. It's what Deacon would have done. "During our marriage, my wife wasn't untrue to me. Since you're a crook, a thief, a swindler and a liar, it's no surprise she chose me instead of you. It shows her good sense. Don't dirty Annie's name again. If you do, I'll kill you."

Ned didn't look frightened. "You'll not hear mean words from me about Annie," he agreed in a thick Irish brogue. "She was a fine colleen. Now as for the miscreant she married, I've no such hesitation in naming him a swine."

"What's your real name?" Deacon asked gruffly.

Ned smirked at him and then straightened in his saddle, tilting his head arrogantly.

"Edward Donovan Tolliver, one generation transplanted from Calgary County in the Old Country, fifth in the Tolliver line to carry me name. There's many a fine Irish lad who's trod the boards and been forced to use his wits to find a meal," he delivered his introduction and excuse for being a reprobate.

"You're an actor?"

"And a fine one," Ned answered proudly. If he could have taken a bow, Deacon was sure he would have. As it was, even with his arms cuffed behind and riding a horse, he conveyed majestic arrogance.

"Beauregard picked up your trail. Where did you slip up?" Deacon made his question sound casual. Half the lawmen in the state were looking for the men passing bad money and the kid had found one of them.

"I saw Beauregard in the tent show where I performed as a traveling minister." Ned dropped his pose and grimaced. His expression changed to piety.

"Brother McCallister, forgive without punishing, trust without wavering, give without sparing. Turn loose this humble soul and let him redeem himself on his knees..."He paused, licked his lips and looked pointedly at Deacon's groin.

"I thought you were partial to women not men." Deacon ignored the offer and snipped the end from a cigar, preparing to light it.

"Figured it was worth a try since you spent the night with Lyd's butler." Ned shrugged. Seeing that his plan to seduce Deacon had failed, Ned nonchalantly continued his original story.

"In Dodge, I had to quit the part of Reverend Landau earlier than I was supposed to because of him." Ned grimaced. "I'd seen that same big, rangy kid with a wolf by his side, lurking around at the Dodge stockyards when I was playing Syms, the banker buying cattle."

Deacon kept his mouth shut, swallowing his astonishment at this revelation. Beauregard had figured out Ned's pattern, recognized the counterfeiter in spite of his disguises and set up a trap to catch him. Good God, the Pinkertons and

Texas Rangers with all of their resources combined were chasing after three nonexistent men.

"Well, I'll be damned," Deacon muttered.

Ned Tolliver, if that was his real name, slid in and out of characters so easily he could have been acting yet again. He'd used his talent, changing identities as he spread fake money in the Texas towns he visited.

Deacon struck a lucifer and lit his cigar, thoroughly enjoying the taste as he inhaled deeply. The drag of depression that thoughts of his late wife and marriage had raised dissipated as he considered what he'd just learned.

Studying the burning tip of his cigar, Deacon focused on the convoluted story Ned was telling. Lydia was right. Beauregard was smart. He was also privy to information Deacon wanted. So before Lydia hired the kid and sent him chasing after more counterfeiters, Deacon wanted his own answers.

As Calvin the butler, the kid had rerouted Lydia's *someone special* to another room. That being certain, it was logical to assume Beauregard had substituted the mystery woman. Why he'd done that was yet to be established, but Deacon intended to find out.

It was a toss-up in his mind which he'd enjoy more — shaking the kid until Beau gave up the name of Deacon's Pleasure Dome bed companion or delivering the news to Beauregard that he wasn't collecting the fifteen hundred dollar reward money for Ned until he answered Deacon's questions.

Until recently, Deacon had made it a practice to mind his own business and keep to himself. For years, he'd had no interest in anything other than the hunt — and that was more about avoiding boredom than delivering justice. Then the Tennessee miscreant had come to Texas, bringing entertainment to Deacon's lackluster life. With both Sam and Charlie married and retired from bounty hunting, Deacon had probably focused more on the kid than he should have.

There'd been plenty of times in the last year Deacon's disagreements with Beauregard had escalated into yelling matches in front of law offices. If there was one person who could bring him roaring to life in a moment, it was the Tennessee Whip.

That was the nickname the outlaws had nailed onto the kid and it fit him well. But Deacon preferred his own nickname for the pest — *Trouble*.

He didn't doubt for a moment that he could coerce the kid into helping him find the woman. The brat was a greedy fool who took unthinkable risks to collect bounty rewards far smaller than the current prize of fifteen hundred dollars.

On the one hand the kid's daredevil attitude had saved Deacon's life. Beau had taken out an outlaw stronghold with the help of a woman. On the other hand, the jackass was barely old enough to be out of the schoolroom, let alone traipsing around the countryside hunting murderers and risking his life.

As usual the thought of Beauregard's audacity made him grit his teeth. He bit off the end of the cigar before he knew what he was doing.

God Almighty, the kid dressed up like a butler and fooled Lydia and everyone else. Deacon wondered how long the young bounty hunter had been employed and how long he'd maintained his disguise.

Obviously Beauregard had fooled Deacon too. His only memory of the butler was of the good quality suit he'd been wearing.

"Since it's not the butler but a woman you're mooning over, as soon as I get free, I'll show her a good time." Ned interrupted Deacon's thoughts with an insult. Evidently, he thought another attempt at rousing Deacon's temper was in order. "It shouldn't be that hard to steal her from you."

"Then I'll have to make certain you don't get loose, Ned." Deacon ignored Lydia's brother, thinking about the woman instead. He'd not had time to bathe before he left this morning and her scent clung to him, tantalizing him with memories of what they'd done.

He'd find the woman from the night before and make things right with her. He didn't know what that entailed. She'd been innocent, shy, bold and lusty all at the same time. His cock stirred, reminding him that it wasn't beneficence driving his pursuit.

Just as much as he wanted to find her, he anticipated the immediate pleasure he'd get from sparring with Beauregard when he arrived in Eclipse. Deacon didn't know what came next but for the first time in years he anticipated the future.

Before they arrived at Eclipse, Deacon turned on the path leading to the MC3. Ned wasn't as happy to be revisiting the McCallister ranch as he'd implied.

"I thought you were taking me to the Eclipse jail," he protested.

"Not this trip," Deacon replied. "There's a matter of a thousand dollars and two appaloosa horses to be resolved. I think you need to visit with my brother Sam and his partner Dan Hawks for a while."

Chapter Four

Miri traveled fast riding Possum's easy trot. The rocking motion made her breasts sway and rub against her clothes. She'd been in a hurry this morning and even had she found time to bind her bosom when she'd pulled on her butler clothes, she wouldn't have because her right nipple was sore—abraded where Deacon had suckled her, turning her into a writhing ball of frenzy.

She flushed, automatically squeezing her thighs together as she remembered the feel of lips and teeth on the tender nub. Possum took her reaction as a signal to speed up and the faster trot forced Miri to tighten her knees and settle her butt deeper in the saddle to keep from bouncing.

The sensitive area between her legs chafed against her clothes and Possum's faster pace slapped the saddle against Miri's private parts, intensifying the burning sensation in her sex. None of her female areas seemed quite right this morning.

"Women have been coupling with men since the beginning of time. I will survive," she murmured out loud. It seemed odd to her the way she could still feel the imprint where Deacon's body had covered hers.

She recalled the shuddering climaxes she'd experienced as Deacon thrust in and out of her. A blush sizzled through her, scalding her cheeks and rolling upward until even the roots of her hair seemed coated in fire.

"God Almighty," she whispered. *No wonder people like to fornicate.* She'd wanted to know about such things, but now she wasn't sure what to do with her knowledge. Her thoughts about Deacon McCallister had subtly changed over the time she'd known him.

From the start she'd spied on him when he didn't know it. He was so darn serious she couldn't resist deviling him when she got the chance. Underneath his somber presence she'd discovered a sharp mind and soft heart. *The preacher man's a* firecracker for sure but he means well when he's bein' bossy.

~ ~ ~ ~ ~

In late August, she'd been in Sundown coming out of the sheriff's office when Deacon had arrived in a rage. Instead of dismounting and going in like any normal person would, he'd ridden his horse up on the boarded walk and blocked her path.

"Hold it right there, Trouble." He'd been a mite perturbed that she'd swooped in and captured one of his wanteds after he'd tracked the man.

The name he called her made her laugh inside. This time he'd been riled more than usual. She wasn't one for backing down, so she'd opened her side of the conversation with a taunt. "Hope yer huntin' went well, McCallister. Mine sure did."

"Get the hell off the sidewalk, McCallister." The sheriff had come out of his office to see what the fuss was.

"When I'm ready." Deacon had been snarling mad and turned his wrath on the Sundown sheriff. Miri had sneaked a glance at Deacon's face while he was looking at the lawman. She'd seen a vein thumping in his forehead hard enough to draw her attention.

"You might want to drink a cup of green tea with some honey in it, Deacon. It's good for calming the nerves." She'd not expected her suggestion to be greeted with thanks but it served its purpose. He'd turned away from the sheriff before the other man shot him, and redirected his anger at the true target—her.

"You swooped in and nabbed Bennett Sawyer after we tracked him to that cabin."

"Try to keep it down, you two." Like any man of good sense, the sheriff hadn't really wanted to quarrel with Deacon. Besides his quick temper, the bounty hunter was known for his fast draw. After delivering his request, the lawman retreated into his office and shut his door.

Ketchum had joined the fray, growling at Deacon's horse and, not being as well-trained or well-mannered as Possum, it started dancing all over the sidewalk, making it hard for Deacon to continue his rant. The distraction had encouraged her to be bold. She'd dropped her voice to its lowest register and thickened her drawl into her best twang. She might have been a little too smug when she'd mocked him.

"He was easy pickins, Deacon. Thanks." She'd been chortling at her accomplishment, ready to brag about how she'd caught Sawyer.

"Bennett Sawyer was a cold-blooded murderer. Are you stupid? You don't need to be facing killers on your own."

"Heck it weren't nothin' catchin' him. He saw you fellers ridin' on and was all set to do a flit and hide again. Good thing I was there to fetch him back to the sheriff."

She'd bragged about the way she'd caught Bennett using the whip, disarmed and cuffed him and hoisted him over a horse while Ketchum stood guard.

"Now that was the hard part," she'd chuckled, admitting the truth. "Sawyer wasn't so tall, but he was a heavy 'un."

"Do. Not. Follow. Us."

For the sake of the thumping vein in his head she'd edged off of the sidewalk and started on her way.

"You heard me, Beauregard. You won't get any more warnings," he'd yelled after her.

And she couldn't keep her lip buttoned. "Well, as to that," she'd answered, "our trails might cross again sometime. I'd count on it, 'twas it me."

She'd almost reached the hitching post and Possum when he brought his horse alongside her again. Finally she'd fumbled a cigarette and lit it, trying to look unconcerned. Orneriness had taken over and she'd puffed the smoke at him. It was a mistake.

"You insolent pup, I've a mind to—" He'd been fit to be tied. Ketchum mounted a rescue, nipping at his mount's heels, sending Deacon's horse dancing sideways. She'd taken it as a sign it was time to skedaddle and climbed on Possum.

"Stay out of my way in the future, brat," he'd called after her. "You're not old enough to shoot but by damn you're not too old for me to turn over my knee and fan your ass."

"Think you can do it, just give it a try." His threat to wallop her fanny had made her body clench and not from fear. She'd ridden away laughing at Deacon and thrown a parting taunt at him over her shoulder. "Until that time I reckon we'll stay in touch."

~ ~ ~ ~ ~

Well we've sure been in touch. The thought of Deacon's wrath if he ever found out she'd been fooling him all along wiped the smile right off her face. Lord knows she'd spent enough time dodging his scrutiny whenever he'd gotten too close.

Might be time for me to find another place to hunt. But that thought depressed her spirits. She liked Eclipse. Maybe after this trip to deposit her promissory note, she'd stay clear of Eclipse for a spell. She frowned. She wasn't sure how long it took for a man to forget about his coupling experience but didn't think it would be more than a week or two.

Probably more like a heartbeat or two. She snorted. As for her, she didn't foresee a time when she wouldn't get warm just thinking about Deacon's body.

Under his beard and dirty clothes he's a handsome devil. And he'd been nice. He'd been sweet to her when it had hurt there at the start. He'd been harder than a steel rod and hotter than a poker but if she'd said "Get off," Miri was certain he'd have climbed down.

It didn't do for her to ponder too long about it because thoughts of Deacon left her flushed and flustered. She had business to conduct before she could daydream.

"I've got a note to cash in for fifteen hundred dollars. I knew I could catch that counterfeiter. I just wish I'd been able to find the printing plates too."

Eclipse was a day's ride from Fort Worth so Miri had plenty of time to think about her Hell's Half-Acre experience. She tried not to get too proud, but heck, anybody could see that tracking, trailing, analyzing and outthinking the wanted counterfeiter was no small thing. *I found Jackson when plenty of others, even government agents, weren't able.*

Though she traveled at a fast clip, she regularly stopped to give Possum a breather. As she and Ketchum walked her gelding, she delivered a running analysis of her experience with Deacon McCallister.

"I 'spect when Deacon gets up this morning he'll be glad I took myself off to other places." She delivered this pithy opinion in her thick Tennessee twang.

"Doubtful," she answered herself in Calvin's voice, enunciating each word thoughtfully. "He said he was taking you out of a den of iniquity today." She carried on her two-sided conversation, pausing every once in a while to get her wolf's opinion.

"What do you think about Deacon, Ketchum? Will he be glad we left or inconsolable that he doesn't get to save this soiled dove today?" Ketchum sat down, his tongue lolling out as he stared at her and grinned.

"Up close he's better looking than even I thought." As she talked to her pet, her voice fell into a soft Southern cadence without the harsh overlay she added when she played Beau.

"There's no sense in worrying about it. It's done and if I could undo it I wouldn't." She grinned wryly at Ketchum and fell back into Beau's voice. "He's mighty fine. His arm muscles make mine look darn right puny."

Her grin melted into a dreamy-eyed smile and her voice changed again when she whispered, "His hair, once I got all the dust and dirt out of it, was a real pretty reddish brown. His beard was darker, but oh my, he's handsome when he shaves it off."

When she let herself think about the night with him, her stomach clenched and hot waves of anxiety made her sweat, though the day itself was cool. She wasn't fool enough to think Deacon McCallister was a man to trifle with. But men didn't care about the women they hired for pleasure and she figured he wouldn't be surprised if the prostitute was gone when he woke.

"Less embarrassing that way," Miri said to Ketchum.

Midmorning, when Miri's stomach began to rumble, she complained out loud. "Most of the Pleasure Dome all-nighters rise late and have breakfast sent to the room." She squinted at the slant of the sun. "I imagine Deacon is getting up about now." She sighed. "Wish I was eating the chef's ham omelet instead of gnawing on a cold biscuit."

She remounted, dug two of the same from her saddlebag and tossed one to Ketchum, then made a face at him. "As soon as we cash in that promissory note, we'll treat ourselves." *I'll buy myself a big chunk of honeycomb to eat during the holidays.*

* * * * *

It was already evening when Miri rode into Eclipse. She stopped at the livery stable and rented a stall for Possum. After she'd groomed, grained and watered her gelding she headed for the sheriff's office, eager to tell Sheriff Potter about catching Ned Jackson. The bank was closed and it would be ten in the morning before she could deposit her note. Hiram was in his office and welcomed her inside, but it didn't take much of a conversation with him to ruin her day.

"Fella at the bank brought this over. He figured I'd see you before you made a trip over there." The sheriff delivered the bad news in the form of a telegram from the Fort Worth sheriff. "Payment to Beauregard voided. Prisoner released."

Miri felt ill. She'd devoted all summer to the hunt, passing on a lot of easier quarry for the bigger prize Jackson offered. Worse yet, she'd invested funds in the butler's disguise. Instead of being flush with money at year's end, she was nearly broke with no way to recoup her loss other than immediately hitting the trail again.

"Let me take a look at what's in your stack of posters, Sheriff Potter." She hid her distress, playing it off as just another one of the ups and downs of bounty hunting.

But he steered her to a chair and handed her a cup of coffee. She wanted to howl in disbelief. She pulled out the promissory note and read it again. Everything had been fine up to the time she'd left.

There had been no doubt in her mind that she'd nabbed the right man. Her prisoner was the counterfeiter. Now he was loose again. She sighed and set the cup down.

Hiram picked it up and put it back in her hand. "One night won't make a difference," he told her. It would and they both knew it. Jackson would be long gone and wearing a new identity when he surfaced again.

"I guess I have some repairs I could do." She had a crumpled white shirt with a button missing. "Might you have some thread and a needle?"

Hiram seemed glad she was staying and hustled to get the sewing tools. "I've only got this white spool of thread," he apologized.

"Guess my luck is improving already because that's just what I need." She smiled gamely, glad he didn't ask what had happened to the button.

"The jail's empty and no one's using the cots. Stay here tonight if you want. Unless someone has a prisoner to deliver, and that's not likely, you should be undisturbed until morning. If someone wants me, I'll be at the hotel."

He gave her the cell keys and left. She barred the door and removed the layers of clothing she wore, using the pail of water in the corner to wash up before she brushed off Calvin's Hutchinson suit and sewed on the button Deacon had cut from the shirt.

"There, good as new," she told it and patted the front. Maybe she could sell the suit at a dry-goods store. It had cost too much to let it lay fallow.

She washed the white shirt, trying not to remember why she loved it and why it was practical to sell it with the suit. By the time she'd hung up her laundry, Miri was bone tired. She'd been on strict mental alert for weeks. Her time at the Pleasure Dome had been particularly difficult since Calvin had been a new identity for her to master.

She sighed. At least the role of Calvin had been a change. She'd studied the clerk at Osgood's when she'd purchased her suit and copied his accent and mannerisms. It had worked and voila, she had another character in her repertoire.

Miri's knack for mimicking voices and such came in real handy. She admitted that she'd played Beauregard so often, had she not caught a glimpse of Deacon McCallister occasionally, the unused feminine part of her would have dried up and blown away on the Texas wind.

Pensively Miri brushed the snarls from her hair, thinking about what she'd done with the other bounty hunter. A wry grin twisted her lips. *I tricked him into having carnal relations with me, that's what I did.* Shame scorched her cheeks as she admitted that without chicanery she'd never have gotten to experience his touch.

Well then I'm glad I cheated, she thought grimly. Growing up half wild and on her own the way she had, she'd kept her eye out for males of interest, figuring that someday she'd find one who suited her. When she'd clapped eyes on the red-haired bounty hunter the first time she'd darn near swooned.

Wearing the shirt she'd earlier stolen from him, Miri lay down on the cot. All day she'd focused on work, waiting for bedtime to savor her previous night's experience. Now that she could, her mind tiptoed around the events, not sure which to explore first.

He said my skin felt like silk. She snorted at that idea, holding her rough calloused hand in front of her eyes as evidence of Deacon's mistake.

Miri closed her eyes and slid her hands under his shirt and up her ribs to cup her breasts. Her lips curved in a smile, remembering the way Deacon's chest hair had tickled her nipples. They ached, sore from his lusty attentions.

She'd never thought of her breasts as anything but a nuisance. Caressing them as if for the first time, Miri admitted she was almost proud of the plump mounds now that she knew Deacon like them.

He kissed and suckled 'em somethin' fierce. Miri caught one stiff bud between finger and thumb and squeezed the pebbled end, wincing at the pain that was both good and bad. Hastily she wet her finger before circling the taut peak with liquid heat. Remembering the feel of his mouth, her back arched and she thrust her breasts high as if reaching for his pleasure again.

Dammit, I'm lying on the jail cot aching with want for him all over again. Miri groaned, the sound a reminder of the previous night's grunts and moans and sighs. She'd thought having her way with Deacon once would end her silly yearnings. Instead, she curled in misery, staring at the bars on the window and knowing that she'd had her taste and it wouldn't happen again.

He wanted me. She knew he had from the way his manhood had stood stiff and ready. The idea excited her so much her hand clenched as if closing around his engorged erection.

Her other hand drifted to her belly, feeling again the pressure of his hard body rubbing against hers. Need clawed in her chest, making it difficult to breathe as she pictured their naked lengths tangled together. Thinking about the night before was a mistake. Heat coiled in her womb and her nerves tightened against frustrated desire.

She relented and tried to ease her torment. Tentatively she slid a finger down the crease separating the lips of her sex. Her feminine folds were drenched in liquid at the thought of having Deacon McCallister again. She cupped one of her breasts, pinching the nipple until a whimper of pleasure escaped her lips.

She rotated her finger, pressing on the nubbin of nerves at her apex and sending tingles of sensation skittering up her spine. Her womb flexed, silently asking to be filled again. Her ministrations weren't enough. She rubbed the sensitive knot the way Deacon had and squeezed her nipple even harder.

Miri pictured her hands sliding through Deacon's pelt as he leaned above her. She tucked her chin beneath the shirt collar, burying her nose in the fabric to add his scent to her memory, wishing she could preserve the smell forever.

He put his hand under my rump and lifted me. Her hips came off the cot and followed the bliss her fingers offered. Her pelvis strained upward, thrusting against her own hand until her body

112

clenched and shuddered in release. Collapsed, sweaty and sated after the experience, she felt foolish. Embarrassed at her actions, Miri fell back on a Beauregard story.

"I 'spect that was what the nuns warned us fellers about." She snorted at her own joke. Though remembering made her grin, she had to be her own audience since she had no one to share the memory with.

At one of the stops on her way to Texas, she'd been playing a male when she attended a Louisiana school run by nuns. The good women had herded the schoolboys to a meeting with the priest and Miri, dressed as Beau, had been included when the nuns instituted the roundup. The priest had explained to the boys that touching their male organs for any reason but pissing was wrong.

He'd stared at them all real hard and said if they'd been frigging themselves, when they went to confession they needed to apologize to God and not do it anymore.

The nuns had been more direct. They'd claimed when boys touched themselves for pleasure, hair grew on their palms. Silly as Miri had thought that warning, after her current experience with carnal pleasure, she checked her hands for signs of fur.

By the slant of the moon, she could tell it was well past midnight and she was still awake, wasting her time whining. She was hungry and she wanted coffee. There wasn't any food to be had, but Hiram had coffee beans in a can.

She swung to her feet and went to the bucket, washing before smoothing the wrinkles from Deacon's shirt.

"Damn," she muttered, staring at the dirty water and weighed the pros and cons of going to the town well for clean.

Might as well lock up here, drop the key to the jail off at the hotel where Hiram is staying and be on my way. But another part of her was so bone-weary she felt incapable of moving from the sheriff's office back to the outlaw trail.

A loud hammering on the door interrupted her indecision. Miri tucked her hair up high before pulling on her shaggy brown wig. Quickly she donned her buckskin pants and let Deacon's shirttails hang long as she padded to the door, unbarring it and swinging it open. And there he was.

"Deacon," she managed to drawl without stammering. "Kinda early in the day for a visit." Her spirits moments before had been lower than a dog's belly, but suddenly they soared. She felt her lips curve into a playful grin that turned into a scowl when he glared at her.

"I figured I'd find you here," he growled.

"I'm playing deputy for Hiram tonight. What's it to you?" She opened the door and then, suddenly aware that she was bareheaded and revealing way too much of Beau's features, she grabbed her hat off Hiram's desk and clapped it on her head.

She needn't have worried. He wasn't looking at her. He'd crossed to where she'd left Calvin's butlering suit. And he was staring at the half-dry ruffled shirt hanging beside it.

It was difficult keeping her expression innocent since the last time he'd seen the shirt, she'd been wearing it and other than that had been naked.

"Hiram's at the hotel," she volunteered. "I'll go get him." She was still sock footed and planned to flee sans boots. She hadn't made it through the door when Deacon stopped her.

"Hold up there. I need to talk to you."

"About what?"

"Any coffee makings?" He walked away from the suit and looked around hopefully.

"What do you want to talk to me about?"

"First off, thanks again for saving my life." Her smile hadn't completely formed when he added, "Second, what in hell are you doing risking your friend's life? Twice now you've sent her into danger. Dammit, Beauregard, do you have any idea what could have happened to her in Pettigrew's camp?"

"She earned her share of the payout same as you. I don't think my business with Miri is any business of yours. As a matter of fact, she was helping me catch another wanted when she ran into you."

"Ned Jackson."

"Yep. So how do you know about him?"

"Suppose I could tell you where to find him again?"

Miri felt the blood in her veins chill. Deacon's smug expression didn't bode well. Outrage swelled in her chest.

"If you know where he is, then you got him out of the Fort Worth jail. Why would you do that? He's worth fifteen hundred dollars to me."

"He's worth a hell of a lot more than that if we can find the plates being used to print the fake money. I've talked to the government men.

Jackson's small potatoes compared to the real quarry."

Miri grabbed the bucket, glad to get out of the office and away from Deacon. She had to resist the temptation to hit him in the head with the pail. She took her time at the town pump, reminding herself that in spite of his arrogance and high-handed manner, he'd done her more than one favor.

Criminy. I saved his life. That ought to count for something. Plus, he was the man who had become her lover even if he didn't know it.

Deacon lounged in the sheriff's office doorway, and she could feel his gaze on her when she returned with the water. Her pulse fluttered wildly.

Ketchum trotted up and butted her free hand so she would scratch his head. She quit what she was doing, set the bucket on the boardwalk and grabbed her wolf around the neck.

"You mangy beast, did you check on Possum this morning?" Ketchum rumbled a mock growl before licking her chin. She rubbed her face against his fur, scratched behind his ears and then stood.

"Better rest up for the hunt, buddy. Thanks to the no-account thieving varmint blocking the sheriff's door, we'll be on the trail again today."

Done with his morning greeting, Ketchum disappeared into the alley, leaving Miri alone in the shadow but for Deacon. He stood in the doorway watching her.

"How old are you, kid?"

"Old enough to recognize shenanigans when I see 'em," she answered, warming up to her complaint. Now that Deacon was here, her distress had been replaced with a mix of anger and relief. "I left my prisoner locked up in the Fort Worth jail for the U.S. marshal to certify. Sheriff Tully turned Ned loose. Now you claim you know where Ned is, which means you stole my catch and stashed him somewhere. Some things appear to be a mite out of kilter in this picture."

Miri stopped in front of him, waiting for him to move rather than squeeze by him in the narrow doorway. Aside from Hiram, he was one of the few people significantly taller than her. She knew her disguise was good from the front and back, but from the top she wasn't so confident. Nor up close if she had to brush against him to get by.

"You smell like that damn wolf." He leaned close to her and sniffed.

The female part of her was appalled. She was having a difficult time staying in character. A dormant feminine side of her nature always fluttered to life around Deacon and the fact that she was close enough for him to inhale her scent and she smelled like Ketchum upset her. She gritted her teeth and mustered her best Beau snarl.

"Yer crowding me, McCallister. Make up yer mind if'n yer in or out, but whatever ya do, move."

"That's my shirt," he muttered and withdrew from the doorway only to catch the tail of her shirt as she scooted by. "Where did you get my shirt?"

"It fell out of the sky and hit me on the head," she answered and pulled free. Miri wrapped herself in Beau's persona as she put the coffee on to perk, then turned to face Deacon, prepared to talk business.

"Spit it out, McCallister. What's yer angle? If you were gonna cash in on Ned, you'd already have done it. But you didn't because he's my catch."

"Nope. Harold Tully was shocked to discover you'd disregarded the Pleasure Dome's neutrality and turned him loose. I wouldn't go back to Fort Worth for a time if I was you."

"I didn't tell Harold squat when I dropped Jackson off. Let me guess, you decided to fill in the gaps of Sheriff Tully's knowledge."

"I always think it's best for all players to know what's going on. And I'll ask one more time. Where did you get my shirt?"

She couldn't very well jerk it over her head and hand it to him because she hadn't bound her breasts. It was a quandary. She shouldn't have kept the shirt, she sure shouldn't have worn it and now she was caught trying to explain it. Attack seemed the only option.

"You are dumb as well as greedy, McCallister, if you think this is done. After I saved your miserable hide, I spent six weeks tracking him." She didn't really have to pretend outrage when she thought of all the time she'd spent following her quarry.

"Don't know why," he drawled. "It took me less than an hour to catch him. You must be doing something wrong, Beauregard."

Least said soonest mended. And I need to skedaddle on out of here. She ignored the taunt, filled two mugs with coffee and handed one to Deacon. "What's yer game?"

He didn't seem in any hurry to conduct business. She remained impassive, refusing to unbend and give him the satisfaction of argument.

"Good coffee. Strong enough to grow hair on your chest," he said. Almost casually he returned to her age with a compliment. "I'd say you're not old enough for this business but you've managed to cut a chunk for yourself." He saluted Miri in appreciation.

"I'm old enough to spot a snake in the grass before I step." Miri dodged his question for the second time by being surly.

"Simmer down. I have to admit you did a fine job of tracking the counterfeiter." Deacon pulled up a chair, straddling it as he faced her.

Since it wasn't like McCallister to heap praise on his competition, she viewed him with suspicion and shrugged.

"Sit down. Let's talk." He tipped his hat to the back of his head before resting his arms on the chair.

She edged farther from him, leaning her shoulders against the wall and standing nonchalantly with folded arms. He locked gazes with her in a staring contest that mocked his earlier show of civility. She noted the stern slant of his lips before he spoke.

"I want her name and where she lives." His words caught her off guard, since they'd been tussling over the counterfeiter.

"Who?" She stalled for time.

"You know who. The woman you sent to my room. Don't lie or I'll wash your mouth out with soap. I already talked to Lydia."

Wash my mouth out with soap? How old does he think I am? Miri caught back the gurgle of laughter threatening to erupt and turned it into a snort.

"I 'spect Lydia loves talkin' to ya. Myself, I spent my time at the Pleasure Dome avoiding Lydia."

"Don't change the subject," Deacon said gruffly. "When you were posing as Lydia's butler, you sent a woman to my room. I want to know where I can find her and you want to know where the counterfeiter is staying. Seems like a fair trade to me."

"Why?" Miri hedged. This was a strange how do you do. She didn't think men normally wanted to know the women they'd used in whorehouses.

At the same time she preened, mentally fluffing her fledgling feminine feathers, she recognized the absurdity of his request. It really wasn't feasible for Beauregard to introduce Miri to Deacon.

But then again, why not? The humor of the situation threatened to send her into peals of laughter. For once she definitely had the upper hand in dealing with Deacon McCallister.

Chapter Five

Deacon wanted to tan Beauregard's hide. Payback was hell. The kid knew he had him over a barrel and he was deliberately stalling. And to add icing to the cake, the brat was wearing Deacon's shirt.

"What do you mean, why?" Deacon growled, his patience stretched thin. Beauregard blew on the hot coffee and then lounged against the far wall, sipping it.

"Why do ya want her name now? Did ya not introduce yerself afore ya had yer way with her?"

Heat scorched up Deacon's neck to burn his ears. The brat sauntered to the coffee, poured himself a cup and took a sip before he answered his own question.

"Well, then, Deacon, it seems like she didn't want ya to know her name if you asked and she didn't say."

"You just point me in the right direction. I'll change her mind."

"Nope. Can't be giving out information about my friends to just any hooligan who comes along." The kid was shaking his head before Deacon got the final words out.

"So you admit she's your friend?"

"From time to time we've helped each other. I'll have to see if she's interested in meeting you again. Meanwhile, I want to question my prisoner." Beauregard's expression was determined.

"Name first. Then I'll see about an interview with Ned."

"Miri," she snapped. "Now where is Ned and when can I question him?"

"Ned's on the MC3. I'll arrange a visit with him after I've met with Miri."

"Not until I've asked her. She might not want to meet with a lowdown polecat who's swindled a friend of hers."

"If Miri is such a good friend, why in hell did you steer her to the Pleasure Dome? You ought to have your ass kicked for such a thing." Rage boiled inside him at the miscreant's poor treatment of his friend.

"She said she was thinkin' of going into the trade and wanted me to fix her up with a customer." Beauregard's drawl deepened. "I was all set to talk her out of it when you showed up. I figured if a round with you didn't change her mind, nothing would." The kid walked to the door and opened it as if he was leaving.

"Where are you going? I'm not finished." Deacon wasn't any closer to knowing how to find the woman. Worse than that, Beauregard knew her and could influence her. His jaw clenched at the thought.

"I am. I've got work to do seeing's how my big catch just got thieved from me. Mind your back trail, preacher man." Beauregard left.

"Dammit." Deacon stood in the door watching Beauregard's hasty retreat. He didn't know the kid much better than when he'd first set eyes on him almost two years before.

~ ~ ~ ~ ~

Deacon had been accompanied by his partners—his brother Sam and cousin Charlie Wolf, and he hadn't been interested in anything but picking up the latest dead-or-alive posters from the Abilene sheriff's office for the next hunt.

Usually when the McCallisters arrived, the townfolk scurried inside and peered from cloaked windows. He didn't know if they were remembering what he'd been—Reverend Robert McCallister preaching the gospel in the First Baptist Church every Sunday. It was just as likely they whispered about what he'd become—part of a trio of bounty hunters feared by anyone with sense.

On the day Deacon met Beauregard though, the street hadn't been silent. Deacon had tracked the catcalls and loud insults to a spot in front of the Chester Saloon.

"Boy, I'm talking to you. Don't ignore me." The heckler had been a sawed-off cowboy carrying a bottle of whisky and staggering from too much drink though the day hadn't seen high noon yet.

The lanky figure being targeted had worn buckskins, leather moccasins laced to his knees and a knife sheathed and tied to his thigh. A drooping belt wrapped around his baggy shirt and he'd sported a short-barreled shotgun in an attached holster. As if that wasn't enough protection for ten men, the kid had worn a coiled bullwhip, carrying it looped over one shoulder and hanging to his waist.

Remembering the moment, Deacon still grimaced in disgust at the whip. It had been the favored weapon of his grandfather and all three McCallisters wore scars from the old man's brutal use of it. On the kid it had been particularly ludicrous for both its size and the skill necessary to wield such a thing. Only an expert whipster could unleash the monster and use it effectively, and that sure as hell wasn't the half-grown whelp currently wearing it.

An undeniable aura of *dumb, young and vulnerable* had shrouded the figure under siege. Apparently the local cowboys hadn't been able to resist the lure. Three in particular had decided to humiliate their selected victim. Four less aggressive friends had lounged in front of the store, egging on the trio.

Deacon had turned his horse and stopped to monitor the escalating street ruckus. He'd raked the hell-raisers with his glance, checking faces to see if he held paper on any of them and marking their features to remember.

All the while, the stripling fumbled in his saddlebags, his back turned to the men, ignoring them. Deacon couldn't see the kid's face, but his arsenal of weapons and rough clothes had apparently attracted the hecklers.

Young or not, his attitude added heat to the simmering discord and it seemed clear that shortly the bastards intended to deliver a severe beating to the kid. But the youth had stalwartly ignored the threat.

"There's not much muscle to him but he's not short on grit." Sam had reined to a halt, fanning himself with his hat as he looked with interest at the scene. "Kid might surprise us if he can use even half those weapons he's totin'."

"Doubtful," Deacon had grunted.

"Fool's gonna get his ass kicked but two bits says he takes a couple of yahoos down with him," Sam had observed unsympathetically.

Charlie Wolf had watched the coming entertainment with interest. Finally he'd turned to Sam and flashed an unexpected grin. "A dollar says the kid wins."

"He'll get thumped and you know it."

Deacon remembered how he'd scowled at his partners and tightened his grip on his carbine, ready to draw down on the cowboys if necessary.

"If he survives today, his best hope is to shed most of the gear and learn to use one weapon well. A young squirt armed to the teeth offers a challenge and that's the only invitation fools need to pick a fight."

The focus of his concern had suddenly spun around, emitting a sharp whistle that called a snarling, slavering beast from the alley. At the same time the kid's hand snaked down faster than lightning, retrieving his knife and throwing it, pinning one miscreant to the mercantile wall.

Then, with an almost delicate flick of his wrist, the stripling unfurled the whip, wrapping the end around the neck of the second bully. The third man sprawled on the ground with a wolf growling in his face. In a moment, the kid had changed the odds from one against three to *what in hell happened.*

"Ya'll have a problem?" the youth had drawled, at the same time surveying seven sets of stunned eyes. Showing Deacon that he had enough sense to recognize help at hand, the kid had dismissed possible threat from the three bounty hunters, focusing instead on the rowdies he'd quelled.

"Why you damn hillbilly. Think you can pull that shit in this town? I'll—" The knife-pinned fellow jerked the blade free and reached for his sidearm.

By reflex, Deacon had levered a round in his rifle's chamber, the sound making a statement in the otherwise silent tableau. The cowboy had turned, facing the threat coming from the McCallisters and the kid's shotgun blast had peppered the drunken sod's hip instead of his groin. Yowls of pain had ended the disagreement.

"Brother," Sam said, "I think you just saved that guy's nuts."

Deacon had kept his rifle steady on the other men while one ran to alert the doctor. The rest carried their buddy up the street to have the pellets picked out.

"That fella on the ground looks a mite green around the gills," Sam had murmured.

Indifferent to his former prey, the beast had stood and shook the dust from his fur. The mauled heckler had staggered to his feet and wiped sweat and animal spit from his face, all the time staring at the animal in horror.

"Who the hell is that kid?" Sam had asked.

"I don't know. But when he gets done growing he'll be someone to reckon with." Deacon had looked back to where the boy had been standing.

The pinto gelding had remained tied to the hitching post, flicking flies from its ears and patiently waiting. When they'd reached the sheriff's office, the wolf sat in front of it eyeing them as they stopped at the hitching rail.

Deacon had gazed at the hulking brute purposefully blocking the entrance. Balefully, the enormous beast had glared back.

"Figured the kid for smarter than that. It won't do him much good to lodge a complaint, 'cause those jackasses work for Henley," Sam had drawled. Because Henley ran the area according to his set of rules—the first being that he and his were always right—it didn't pay to get in an argument with the rancher.

"The kid'll be lucky if the sheriff doesn't arrest him." At that thought, Deacon had swung down from his horse, again ready to save the youngster's neck. The wolf had flashed fangs along with a low growl, letting Deacon know he wasn't getting into the office.

"Two bits says Deak can take the lobo. You in, Charlie?" Smooth as silk, Sam had transferred his former bet to the new event.

Deacon had ignored his partners and stepped onto the planking, meeting the wolf's stare. He'd curled his lip and growled back, his hand hovering over his gun. He hadn't wanted to shoot the damn beast, but if push came to shove, he would have.

The animal had stood, stretched as though indifferent to Deacon's presence and lifted his hind leg, urinating on the wall. Then he'd turned, facing the bounty hunters again.

"I'm going in, so get the hell out of the way." Deacon's temper, which had been simmering below the surface, spilled out, challenging the wolf to a fight if need be. He'd prepared himself to argue with the sheriff over the kid, Henley and anything else Johnson brought up. The old lobo had cocked his head sideways as if considering Deacon's words. Then he'd turned aside and flopped down on his belly, resting his head on his paws. He'd closed his eyes as if to say "You're not worth my effort".

Prepared to save the kid, Deacon had walked into the sheriff's office and stalled in the doorway, dumbstruck. The kid had been sitting on the edge of the desk, rolling a cigarette, watching the lawman stack wanted posters.

"Beau here's just gettin' started in this area and I thought I'd show him some hospitality. I gave him his choice of handbills this time." Ed Johnson had glowered at Deacon and spoken defensively.

"Thankee, Sheriff. Aw 'preciate it." The kid's accent marked him as being from somewhere southeast of Texas. He'd made quick work of claiming the posters he wanted, tucking them inside his loose shirt before he'd uncoiled his considerable length, towering half a head above the older man.

The young bounty hunter had shambled across the room to the door and stopped when Deacon blocked his path. The foray outside had whet his interest in what the kid looked like up close.

Though the younger bounty hunter topped most men in height, Deacon was bigger. For some reason he'd wanted the youth to understand that. When Beauregard pulled his hat low, clearly intending to sidle past without words, Deacon remained in his way.

"You'll pay hell if you hang around here. That was one of Henley's riders you peppered with buckshot," he advised.

"Salt," Beauregard had corrected him. "Rock salt that burns like all get-out. I 'spect he won't set a horse easy for a time. But he'll be punchin' cows for Henley come dawn tomorrow."

Deacon had had to clench his jaw to keep his mouth from falling open. Silently he'd stepped aside for Beauregard to leave.

133

~ ~ ~ ~ ~

Swamped with memories of the kid, Deacon stood alone in Hiram's office. He'd bungled his negotiations for the woman's name. His leverage, the counterfeiter, was in Sam's hands. The only restriction Deacon had put on his brother was a request to keep Ned alive until Beauregard could question him.

Deacon scribbled a note telling the sheriff to watch out for Lydia Lynch, set the coffeepot off the stove, emptied his cup and placed it on the sheriff's desk before he started for the door. He stopped, his gaze turning to the fancy suit Beauregard had left behind.

Maybe the kid left a note or name. Deacon searched the pockets and found nothing. He inspected the ruffled shirt, comparing it to the one worn by his bed companion. He fingered it thoughtfully, picturing the way it had fit over her lush breasts. His cock stirred and his breath caught in his lungs.

None of the pearl buttons on this shirt were missing, unlike the button he'd severed using his razor. He set the shirt aside, ready to assume that it was standard wear by Pleasure Dome employees. And then he took it back up. He'd been at the house long enough to see several of Lydia's security patrol during business hours and they'd worn suits, but not ruffled shirts.

Why was Deacon's bed companion wearing a ruffled shirt, the costume a butler like Calvin—Beauregard in disguise—might wear?

Did Beauregard, playing Calvin and wearing this suit, take off his shirt and loan it to her? Deacon scratched his head. It didn't make any sense.

He stared at the buttons on the shirt then at the needle and white thread sitting on Hiram's desk next to his coffee mug.

The butler had on that shirt. The woman I bedded wore that shirt. Now Beauregard is wearing my shirt and my shirt was last seen on the woman I...

"It's not possible."

It surprised Deacon that his hand was steady as he locked the outer door to the jail. His thoughts could only be described as pure chaos. What he'd begun to suspect couldn't be true, but nothing else made sense. After he left the keys with the hotel desk clerk, Deacon headed for the stable at the end of the street.

The kid's horse and wolf were missing but they couldn't be too long gone. He questioned the stable owner who obliged Deacon by telling him in which direction Beauregard had ridden.

"I figured if a round with you didn't change her mind, nothing would." Deacon was reminded all over again he'd bedded a virgin. He was filled with guilt thinking about a young innocent woman losing her maidenhead to his lust—until he considered the possibility that Beauregard was the young woman pretending to be a young man.

After reconsidering the body he'd enjoyed so thoroughly, he could assure himself that Miri, if that was her real name, was indeed a woman.

Stepping judiciously to the next point, Deacon decided that if Miri was in fact Beauregard, the hellion had engineered her own deflowering—a consideration that tempered his feelings of guilt but in no way lowered his determination to...

That was the problem. For a man who'd been navigating life with tepid disinterest, his emotions were in an unmanageable tangle. He was mumbling considerations and arguments of what he should do and riding at a fast clip out of town when Sheriff Potter haled him from the doorway of the jail.

"Hold up there, McCallister."

Deacon changed course to where the sheriff leaned on the doorframe drinking a cup of coffee and frowning.

"Tie up there at the hitching post and come inside. We need to talk." As soon as Deacon obliged the sheriff and they were in his office, Hiram didn't mince words. "What happened in Fort Worth?"

Deacon sketched the basic story, expunging the part where he'd indulged in a night of carnality. He wrapped up his explanation and Hiram began a calm but determined inquisition.

"Is he your prisoner or Beau's?" Hiram asked.

"We're working together on this one," Deacon answered. Then he opened his mouth and his own question spilled out. "What's any of this to you? You have a personal interest in the kid?" Deacon bristled as he considered Hiram Potter.

"That I do," Hiram said agreeably, filling a pipe as he squinted over the bowl at Deacon. It occurred to Deacon that it was a gesture Beauregard had adopted, using cigarettes to stall.

"I like Beauregard. No, let me make it stronger." The sheriff paused as Deacon's frown grew into a scowl. "If Beauregard was my child, I couldn't be any prouder than I am."

Hiram lit his pipe and made a show of extinguishing the lucifer. "Now I'll ask again. What happened in Fort Worth? And don't give me that hooey about partnering unless it's true. I've been

137

worried and my mind would rest a lot easier knowing it was the two of you riding together and not just that young—"

"Woman," Deacon finished for him. "I guess we're skating around what we both know. Beauregard's a woman."

"And you would know this how?" Hiram couldn't have looked more forbidding if he'd held a shotgun on Deacon.

* * * * *

Miri fled Eclipse, unwilling to face Deacon McCallister or entertain any more of his blasted questions. He'd never been one to mince words and from the start of their acquaintance had taken it upon himself to give her instructions.

Upon their second meeting, he'd lit into her with a rough scold. The gist of his complaint had been that the kid—Beauregard—was all set to get himself killed.

"That salt rock ammunition you're using will swell up and explode on you if you're not careful. Keep your gun barrel dry. Better yet, get out of this game. You're not old enough."

"Rock salt's cheap, buckshot's a mite more dear. Reckon I can make do with what I have." She'd shrugged away Deacon's safety tip, tucking her head low while she'd made a beeline for Possum. It didn't matter. The older bounty hunter had walked beside her, seemingly intent on having his say.

"Mind what I said about the ammunition. Buy some buckshot for that sawed-off shotgun you carry and stop using rock salt."

"Yer stickin' yer nose in my business, McCallister. Best mind yer own or I might take a notion to poke around in your'n," she'd answered in her best Tennessee twang, making it clear the young bounty hunter didn't appreciate Deacon's warning.

Playing Beau had become as easy as wearing a second skin—her disguise enabling a lucrative business. As Beau, she'd become a young, shambling country bumpkin who brought in outlaws for a living.

But McCallister had from the first made her feel uneasy. Instead of accepting the character she'd put before him and moving on as most folks did, he'd asked questions and inserted himself into her business—a thing she just couldn't allow.

Irritating her even more had been the astonishing fact that he made her want to tear off her hat and wig and climb on him instead of

Possum. There weren't many men who got her attention unless they had a price on their head, but McCallister had been different. As soon as she'd met him, she'd known he was special. It was in Sundown, during their second meeting, that her heart had pounded like a Kiowa tom-tom when he'd started giving her orders.

"Buy some buckshot," he'd snarled before he turned and stalked away.

Miri had studied him as he'd headed across the street to the sheriff's office. Muscled shoulders topped the strong arms that gave her such a visceral reaction. Her womb had clenched when her glance roved lower, pausing on his rump. She couldn't say why, but she'd liked the way it looked, too. As far as Miri was concerned, that marked the beginning of her unnatural interest in the big red-haired bounty hunter.

She'd probably risked too much in having her way with him, but she didn't care at the moment. She'd finally gotten to touch that fine backside and didn't really think anything could ever make her regret the night before. Not even Deacon's robbing her of her catch.

Knowing better didn't always mean doing better. Miri had been deliberately crossing paths with Deacon since they'd met. She'd even looked forward to his complaints and scolds, though his forceful assault on her whip had caused consternation.

"That whip's nothing but an invitation to trouble. You need to set it aside." He'd accosted her in one of the many towns and insisted the kid listen to him.

"Usually that kind of advice comes from someone who can't use a whip," she drawled. She'd fingered the stock of the weapon she wore coiled over her shoulder. Adding the whip to her bounty hunter costume made sense to her. It was more than a prop since she really did know how to use it. She'd demonstrated her ability in Abilene the first day she'd met Deacon when she'd been putting on her *don't tread on me* show.

"Don't assume you're the only whipster around. You're just the only one stupid enough to get strangled with it."

Before she'd known what to expect, he'd grasped the coiled whip, pulling it taut until the handle pressed against her windpipe.

"I could crush your throat. I had you before you even knew what was happening."

It had been hard keeping her head down while he'd used her own whip to choke her. Since Miri hadn't been able to throw her head back and yell at him she'd leaned in, grabbed his shoulders and kneed him in the groin so hard most men would have been on the ground. He'd shuddered, cursed and released his hold on her. She'd stepped back, breathing hard and rubbing her throat.

"Maybe you can teach me that move sometime, preacher man." She'd retreated fast, sneering the taunt over her shoulder.

"You take too many chances, you young fool. Chances that are going to get you killed."

"No more than you," she'd assured him. Deacon's anger surprised her. *He's a firecracker for sure.* Knowing that fact made it even sillier to taunt him. She'd sauntered away, feeling the heat of his glare all the way through her duster, congratulating herself for having foresight in wearing it. The loose oilskin coat had added another layer to her disguise, which she definitely needed around McCallister.

Deacon's gaze made her nipples turn into hard nubs beneath the tight binding around her breasts even though she willed against her body's response. He'd always made her feel—cocky. At least that's what she called it when the heat coiled in her belly and her hips started to sway like a woman's.

"Catch ya later, McCallister. Mind yer back trail." She'd looked over her shoulder to observe his response and was well pleased to see him clenching his jaw as he'd watched her departure.

Robert, the preacher man with a gun. She'd understood his attack had been meant to teach her a lesson that might save her life. And her retaliation had been meant to show him she could take care of herself. After their encounter in Marrow, Miri figured she and Deacon had been officially introduced and she'd settled in to enjoy knowing him.

She'd chosen the McCallisters to trail because in their own peculiar fashion, they were honorable men, smart enough to learn from and safe to be trusted. She'd quit wearing the whip but she hadn't quit following the McCallisters, especially Deacon.

It had tickled her some the way he'd snapped at the bait every time she'd thrown an insult out to rile him. *Beau gets him slack-jawed and pissin' bullets every time.*

Never mind Beau, Miri had spent many a night remembering the feel of Deacon's shoulder muscles when she'd grabbed him. Even through her gloves

143

she'd felt the power in his arms. It had been only the element of surprise allowing her strike to get through. He'd been mad as a rabid wolf when she'd kicked him in the balls. But he'd still been bellowing about her safety just the same.

We've had some right interestin' discussions, the two of us. She should have avoided him. She hadn't been able to resist seeing him though. And now because she was a ninny, she'd lost her biggest bounty ever to the miscreant.

Chapter Six

Even before Ketchum trotted to Possum's side and sat down, Miri knew they were being followed. Since she preferred knowing who was on her trail, she figured it was time to find out. She camped for the night, built a small fire and made a show of grooming Possum before fading into the surrounding shadows with Ketchum leading the way in their investigation. Any predators lurking in her path scurried away at the approach of the big wolf guiding her.

She and Ketchum were squirming on their bellies on the ground using the twilight and half darkness for cover when her quarry struck a lucifer and lit his cigar.

"Lose something?" Deacon drawled.

Miri felt like a fool. Ketchum growled at the same time his tail thumped. Evidently her wolf couldn't decide whether to bite Deacon McCallister or lick him. Miri had the same problem. She stood and brushed the dirt off her buckskins before she answered in Beau's voice, "You followin' me fer a reason, McCallister?"

"I decided to hold back from coming into your camp for the night until you'd made a fire and put the coffee on. Catch."

Miri caught the jack he tossed.

"I brought supper. You cook."

"Maybe I don't want company."

"Get used to it. Until we find the counterfeiter's plates, we're partnering." Deacon delivered his astonishing opinion before he grunted and rode past her toward her camp, leaving her standing in the dark holding a dead rabbit.

"Ketchum," she muttered in her best Beau voice, "I think we're looking at trouble. What say you?" The big wolf whined, nudging the rabbit in her hand and reminding her to get moving. Now this was a quandary for certain. She'd ridden away to put distance between her and Deacon McCallister and he'd followed her.

I don't think I can sleep across from him and not crawl into his bedroll. She groaned. Dammit, she'd been planning on stretching out by the fire and reliving her Pleasure Dome experiences. Now here was the real-life version of Deacon stomping all over those plans as he bullied his way into her camp, dogging Beauregard's heels and impeding Miri's happy dreams.

Her theory that one taste of Deacon would be enough was not proving true. She swallowed, trying to tamp down her lust. Reminding herself to focus on reclaiming Ned, she returned to camp.

Deacon had removed his saddle and was brushing down his horse when she and Ketchum entered the camp.

"McCallister, you've got a lot of nerve showing up here." She threw the rabbit back at him. "I've got my own food."

"So be it," he agreed amiably enough. He didn't say another word.

Miri pulled her hardtack and jerky from her saddle bags and sat by her fire, daring him to pour himself a cup of her coffee. She was mesmerized by her proximity to the man who simultaneously enraged and aroused her.

She chewed her tough jerky watching as Deacon deftly skinned, cleaned and spit the carcass of the rabbit. Then he set the meat aside to build his own fire and finished grooming his horse as the flames burned low enough for cooking.

Using a metal rod he pulled from his saddle bag, Deacon propped the meat over the coals, rotating the spit and browning the meat on all sides. Juice sizzled as it dropped on the fire. Miri's stomach growled as she watched. It was almost less torture to look at Deacon.

Whiskers had grown back, covering the lower half of his face. The new growth looked more black than red in the half light of camp. She shivered and hunched closer to her fire, remembering how she'd watched him shave his beard off. Desperately she snarled in Beauregard's meanest tone, "McCallister, I don't know what yer up to, but I'm guessing it ain't to my benefit."

"Sure it is, kid. You think too small, Beauregard. I'm going to help you find the plates, catch a gang of counterfeiters and collect the bounty on all of them. In return for my help, you're going to introduce me to the young woman I met at the Pleasure Dome."

Miri choked so hard on her biscuit she spilled her coffee. Deacon crossed the space between them and thumped her back until she wheezed and quit coughing. Then he filled his cup with her coffee, handed her a plate with a piece of rabbit meat on it and retreated to his side of the camp.

Well don't that beat all? I guess he was partial to how it felt too. But I can't very well say hello, Deacon. Nice seeing you again. By the way, I'm a female... It appeared that he was planning to attach himself to her like a leech until she introduced him to his coupling companion.

"I'm heading for Abilene with a stack of Hiram's wanteds." She glared across the two fires at him. "Alone. You've wasted enough of my time. I'm on to other things."

He glowered back, giving her his *don't sass me I'm older than you* stare. It was sure different from the way he'd looked at his Pleasure Dome whore. The thought made her mad for some reason and she glared even harder at him.

"Concentrate on the hunt you're on instead of haring off to pursue the wild bunch in Abilene." He had the nerve to give her advice.

"Outlaws like to drink and carouse with women, and Abilene has plenty of saloons to meet their needs," Miri told him. Of course it was a bonus for the thieves and murderers that the Abilene sheriff made it a point to ignore them lest he be required to make an arrest. "Don't be interfering with my bounty hunting, McCallister," she added when Deacon's frown grew bigger.

Since they had a history of stealing each other's quarry, she knew he understood what she meant. Not only had he just hijacked her prisoner from the Pleasure Dome, but the last time she'd been in Abilene, he'd poached her prize there too.

"Tell me something, Trouble. When you went hunting in Abilene, did you just walk down the boardwalk and peer inside the businesses to see if there was a likely outlaw prospect waiting to be caught?" His drawled question revealed he was thinking about their last bout in Abilene too.

"As a matter of fact, that is more or less how I found Luke Kelly," she answered defensively. She'd arrived and tied Possum to the hitching rail next to a row of saloons and dance halls and made a trip down the boardwalk fronting them, stepping inside and scanning the customers of each bar. She'd expected to see at least one of the faces on the posters in her vest and she hadn't been disappointed.

Luke Kelly had been in the Ace High Saloon. She'd been carrying paper on him for a spell and hadn't needed to pull out her wanted poster to know it was his ugly face she'd been looking at. She'd had an advantage — Kelly didn't know her. It was her plan to surprise him and take him out without leaving him dead.

"McCallister, Kelly was in my sights. You got in my way that day and darn near got your head blown off." As soon as the wanted man had spotted Deacon coming through the saloon doors, he'd gone for his gun.

She shuddered at the memory and glowered at the miscreant across the fire. He glared back, giving her his mean grizzly bear stare. But there hadn't been a thing lumbering or bearlike about Deacon in the Ace High when he'd strode into the saloon and traded bullets with Kelly.

Before she'd been able to blast her quarry with a load of rock salt, Kelly had drawn his weapon. But even as he got off his shot, Deacon's bullet tore a hole in his chest and gouts of blood stained Luke's shirt red. All had taken place in less time than it took to crack an egg.

Paying no heed to her, Deacon had crossed the floor, slung the dead man over his shoulder and left the Ace High. After he'd carted the body to the sheriff's office and collected the money that was rightfully hers, he'd headed for the town livery, continuing to ignore her until she'd stepped in his path.

"I told you to leave the murderers to me." As he had that day, he growled at her now.

And as she had that day, she protested. "You take the juiciest wanteds for yourself."

Suddenly he wasn't across the fire. He was standing in front of her and she was standing facing him and poking him in the chest all over again. "Kelly had a big payout and... He. Was. Mine." She'd glared at him, "I could have—"

"Gotten your head blown off," he roared, making her step back. But then she remembered the circumstance and stepped close again, grabbing Deacon's chin while she traced the scar on his face. Luke's shot had gone wide that day, nicking Deacon's cheek instead of hitting him between the eyes as intended.

"Glad to see the bullet crease healed," she said wryly. "Kelly's bullet came real close to sending ya to meet yer maker, McCallister."

She'd followed Deacon from the Ace High that day, determined to see how bad he was hit. When she was satisfied it was a flesh wound, she'd shoved a slab of honey at him.

"Dab that on the hole in your face and it'll heal it." Examining the scar now, she repeated her words from that day. "I don't see why ya think yer such a dadblamed fine hunter."

"Wasn't anything but a scratch and your remedy healed it fine." He leaned closer to her, his breath brushing across her lips as he held her gaze. His eyes glittered when he stared at her.

"Like I told you that day, everybody knows honey's good for healing." For a moment she had the silly notion he might bite her hand. Hastily, Miri released her grip on his chin and retreated to her spot by the fire.

"I 'spect if I go on to Abilene and corner a likely prospect, yer gonna trail after me and steal my catch away again."

"Yep."

Well, fiddlesticks and damnation. Just as sure as she defied him, he'd trail after her. It didn't do any good to complain. She wasn't going to get loose from Deacon long enough to do some serious bounty hunting. She'd outwit him when she could. Meanwhile, another part of her vibrated at the sound of his voice, the smell of his sweat and the sight of his lips close enough to kiss. She sighed.

You'd think as pigheaded and know-it-all as he is, I'd quit mooning over him. In spite of her anger at his tactics, the female silly part of her was all aflutter because he was sitting across the fire. Not one to let opportunities slip away, she put aside both her animus and attraction.

"All right. Since you won't let me get on with my usual work, let's talk turkey. Did Jackson point you to where we can find the printing plates?"

Finding them and returning them to the government agents was worth more than the bounty on the counterfeiter. Together they equaled a sum bigger than all she'd made the year before. Whatever Deacon knew, she needed to find out too.

"Jackson got chatty on the way to Eclipse."

"Tell me." Miri ground her teeth together to keep from ranting. If she'd had time with Ned the information would have been hers.

"First we agree to share what you know and vice versa."

Miri froze, thinking over his proposition.

"Anything I know about the counterfeiter goes on the table. Anything else I know is none of your business." Finally, after stating her reservations, she agreed.

"It is if it crosses our hunt for Ned, the Pleasure Dome and the people who work there."

She ate the slice of rabbit he'd given her and considered his counterdemand. "Ned never got inside."

"But he was headed there."

"I know that. That's why I was butlering for Lydia Lynch."

"How did you know to expect him there?"

She didn't mind tooting her own horn and relaxed with her coffee, explaining how she'd gotten curious about the phony money being passed from town to town. Since she knew most of the sheriffs and gossiped with all she knew, she'd picked up some interesting facts. A raft of phony ten dollar notes had been circulating through Texas all summer.

She pulled two bills from her pocket, one folded around the other, and stood, walking around the fires to hand them to Deacon.

"Look here," she said, leaning over his shoulder and pointing. "If you turn the bill upside down then the eagle looks like a donkey."

Deacon did an odd thing then. He turned his head as she leaned over him and instead of looking at the bills, he inhaled.

When she jerked upright, moving away from him, he laughed. "Still stink like a wolf, Beauregard. You need a bath."

Relief warred with pride. She'd not wanted him smelling her if somehow it reminded him of their night together. It was a possibility since every time she got close to him, his scent made her toes curl. On the other hand, knowing that she still smelled like Ketchum made her face burn.

She covered her chagrin with a taunt. "That bill's named after you."

"Jackass notes." Deacon studied the twin ten dollar bills and laughed at her remark, drawing her attention back to the money. "I've seen this kind of tenner before. Both bills look the same to me. Which bill is fake and which is real?"

"See that?" She tapped the string of numbers on the bill. "All the counterfeit bills have the same serial number ending in a one and a seven. Other than that, the money's printed on the same paper as the real deal and the bills are the same."

"Better have the clerks and bank tellers armed with a magnifying glass," Deacon growled, returning the two bills to her.

"I 'spect they're looking sharp. Most folks take money pretty seriously."

"How did you come by your sample evidence?" he asked.

"Well, I was in the Dodge sheriff's office picking up a stack of wanteds when this fella came in, complaining and fit to be tied. He'd ridden in late and his herd was small, so he didn't get the attention of the main buyers. He'd sold to a banker named Syms and took payment in crisp one hundred dollar bills."

Miri had felt so bad for the rancher. After all his work he was going home broke. He'd tried to deposit his money and been told his bills were fake.

"The sheriff couldn't help him, other than to take down the description of the banker. I followed him out and bought one of his bills."

"You paid him for the counterfeit money?"

"Yep." Outrage erased her pleasure in storytelling and she lost Beau's accent as she answered Deacon. "Dollar for dollar. He needed the money and I needed a copy of what I was chasing. It seemed only fair." Her drawl became a snarl.

157

"I've invested a pile of money in this hunt and you're costing me my bounty."

"We need to work together," he said calmly.

Miri realized belatedly that she had hold of his shirt and was in his face. Hurriedly she released her grip on the material and stepped back, returning to her blanket. His placid indifference to her anger calmed her fury better than a bucket of water. She didn't have an audience besides Deacon's mount, Possum and Ketchum and there didn't seem any point in arguing. Never one to miss an opportunity for entertainment, Miri spent the next part of the night educating Deacon on the counterfeiting going on.

"According to Hiram Potter's contact with the Texas Rangers, Logan Doyle, Pinkertons were already in Texas tracking the spread of the tens when *whoop-de-do*, suddenly counterfeit one hundred dollar notes started floating into circulation. Some of the stockmen and merchants in Dodge got hit hard."

"Anybody watching our bank?"

"Hiram warned 'em. The Eclipse Bank president said he'd be on the lookout. Comfort Quince has her clerks at the Mercantile checking each ten or one hundred dollar bill against the serial numbers I wrote down for Hiram."

"Tough to track the money with everyone spending this time of year." Deacon looked pensive as he lit his cigar. After blowing out the match, he added casually, "According to Jackson, he was supposed to pick up another batch of phony money while he was at the Pleasure Dome."

"I figured that." Miri wanted to cuss a blue streak. "The coyote traveled under different names but he always ended up at the Pleasure Dome. Lydia Lynch? She's got some fancy bathtubs to pay for." As soon as she mentioned the bathing devices she wished she'd kept her lip buttoned. Deacon tensed noticeably across the way, staring hard at her.

"What." She grimaced at him. "Did you think I worked there and never took a peek into one of her fancy suites?"

"Ever try one of the beds out?" he asked mildly.

"Naw, course not. I was her butler." Of course that wasn't the truth at all. But she sure wasn't going to confess to Deacon that she'd tested one of Lydia's beds with him and could personally testify the tubs were big enough for two.

"A kid your age needs to stay out of places like that," Deacon growled. "You have no sense."

"How old is old enough to visit a flop house?" She couldn't resist asking.

"Older than you, that's for damn sure."

"You visit Lydia's place often?" She tried to make the question casual but couldn't keep the disapproval from her voice. Which was silly because she'd watched Deacon and knew for a fact he didn't visit whores and brothels.

"No, I don't. I only went there this time following the counterfeiter — as you did."

"Then why'd you have yer way with my friend?" She hadn't intended to ask that question. But as soon as it was out of her mouth, she waited with bated breath for his answer.

"Almost seems providential, I'd say," Deacon drawled.

She didn't understand that answer at all but there was something about his tone that kept her from asking him for clarification.

He didn't shoot any more questions at her, making a point of laying his bedroll out to indicate that he was done talking. She thought about jabbering longer just to irritate him, but it had been a long day so she rolled out her own bed, slid under the blanket and stared across the fire, waiting for him to go to sleep so she could listen to him snore again.

Deacon hid his grin. Beauregard did smell a little like a wolf. But the male musk that should have been present on a sweaty young man wasn't there. Instead, Deacon finally recognized why he'd been suspicious of the kid for a year. Beauregard smelled like a woman.

The damn floppy hat with its brim pulled low had disguised her features, the shambling walk, the slouch—as tall as she was, she'd not looked out of place in her settings. She wore loose buckskins, hiding her lithe grace, and added her Tennessee twang to the picture. The disguise was damn near perfect. Only her scent was wrong and she'd taken pains to cover that with the clinging smell of tobacco.

He wanted to ask her what frightened her so much she hid inside men's clothes and hunted devils for safety. But though he'd explored every inch of her body, he wasn't on that kind of personal level with her. She didn't trust him enough to let him know she was female let alone admit she was his Pleasure Dome lover. Hell, he hadn't even gotten past the hat yet.

The two counterfeit bills in his pocket matched hers. He'd gotten his hundred from Sam and his ten from the Texas Rangers. Deacon stared across the fire at the kid. Beauregard's collection of information was impressive. And she'd gathered it alone, sprinkling business talk in with her tall tales as she'd visited with sheriffs from town to town.

Every moment shared with Beauregard erased more of her disguise, allowing Deacon to see what lay beneath. When he taunted her to anger, her Tennessee twang became a husky Southern snarl and she wore an expression of female outrage on her face. How she had managed to fool so many people for such a long time, he couldn't fathom — but it was obvious she had.

"I wouldn't have figured it out the way she keeps bundled up with no skin showing. But her eyes reminded me of a woman I once knew. I guess I looked at her harder and longer than most do," Hiram Potter had admitted.

Deacon still felt a stir of jealousy. Hell, she'd kept her hat brim down and her eyes hidden from him for better than a year.

Add that to the seductive virgin who'd ridden him to completion more times in one night than in all the other sexual encounters he'd had in... He snorted at that thought. Hell, he hadn't had any. He'd been chasing Beauregard's tail whether he'd admitted it or not. Unwilling to let her end the conversation, Deacon sat up on his blanket, interrupting the night's silence with his question.

"Beauregard, what's your business with Hiram Potter?" Possessive, animalistic intent blossomed in his chest. He knew what Hiram had said.

"My interest in her is fatherly. How about yours?" They'd established that Deacon had no paternal feelings toward Miri though he was still stumbling over the idea that the kid he'd been trading taunts with for over a year was his Pleasure Dome companion. His initial impulse to expose her ruse had changed with Hiram's caution.

"Even with her visiting me at the sheriff's office so often, it took me more than a few months to figure out the truth of her being female. When I did, I didn't mention it. If she's hiding from someone, it's not the law. I sent for posters from Tennessee and the states between here and there. She's not wanted. That leaves hiding for another reason. I kind of hope she trusts me enough someday to let me help."

"You Potter's relative?" Deacon nudged her with his question since he didn't have Hiram's patience. Waiting wasn't something he felt inclined to do when it came to meeting Miri again. In his thoughts, the kid and the seductress were still separate entities.

"I decided to adopt Hiram," she drawled. "Havin' no kin the way I do, I'm building my own family."

Deacon tried to imagine what she'd do if he suddenly yelled *Take me, take me.* In spite of the buckskins and the Tennessee twang she used to put distance between them, every nerve in his body strained toward the woman across the fire.

He needed a way to stay close, an excuse to learn more about her and a means to keep her safe. Whether Miss Beauregard knew it or not, the rules had just changed. Before she retreated into hostile silence, he offered his proposition.

"I meant it when I said I want you to partner with me until we finish this job. I'll use what money I have to tide us over if you're short. I've got my own reasons for this hunt. My brother Sam and his partner Dan Hawks lost money the same way that cattleman did. They took cash payment for two appaloosas they sold."

He stood up and walked around the campfire the way she had earlier, and this time, he pulled his bills from his pocket and showed her. "The Pinkertons took their money as evidence but Sam held back half of the bills. That's how I have mine."

"So you let me babble on and already knew all about the counterfeiter." She gave him a disgusted look but he definitely had her attention. He didn't know whether it was from his proximity or his evidence but she sat up on her bedroll and slapped on her hat, holding out her hand for the bills. She unwound, standing gracefully before she shambled away from him to crouch by the fire, using the light to inspect his money.

"The law's still chasing three men. Maybe I can collect triple for Ned if I work it right. As for the plates, I'm doing fine on my own."

"You can't collect triple for one man even if I give him back to you. And you're not going to find the plates on your own. You need help. I'm volunteering."

"Why?"

"I told you. Sam and —"

"Good luck to your huntin'. Myself, I like to work alone." She waved his excuse away and pulled her hat down lower, hunkering by her fire

Beauregard was smart, able to make connections and see patterns. She didn't need him to think for her. But bounty hunting was a dangerous business and regardless of whether or not her disguise was revealed, eventually she was bound to get shot, stabbed, beaten or killed.

Deacon had just spent the better part of a year vetting the damn fool's hunts. Beauregard knew the sheriff in each town—but Deacon knew the lawmen better. He'd made it a point to talk to each man about what posters to show the kid.

It hadn't taken much to convince the lawmen to send Beauregard after swindlers rather than cutthroats although the brat had still claimed more than a few dangerous wanteds. But now…

"I'd like you to contact your friend and tell her I want to meet with her."

"For what?" She was on guard, her voice filled with suspicion. "I asked before, you didn't say."

"I have no intentions of discussing my interest in her with you," he said gruffly. "You just need to understand that I mean her well. I'd consider it a favor if you'd put me in touch with her."

"I'll let her know. Not promising she'll want to see ya, though." The kid didn't sound encouraging but Deacon piled on more reasons to meet the woman again.

"I'll trade you a visit with the counterfeiter, who by the way says he's Lydia's brother and his real name is Edward Tolliver."

His offer got immediate results.

"Done." All business, the kid gathered her bedroll and kicked the embers of her fire out.

"What about my next meeting?" he asked as she crossed to where she'd left her horse ground-tied.

"It's clear to me you've got a bad case of the babbles tonight. I'll spell it out for ya. I'll see my prisoner, talk to him, see if he's got any leads for me. If he does, I might have to chase them and not your lady friend. When time allows, I'll see to the meeting. Understand?"

She swung up on her horse and looked down at the wolf materializing from the shadows. "You ready, partner?"

Beauregard's twang was in place and she was moving fast in the direction of the McCallister ranch. Evidently Deacon's offer of a joint venture had been rejected and she preferred partnering with the mangy wolf loping by her side.

Chapter Seven

Miri wanted to talk to Ned and get on with her business. It was fine taunting Deacon from across a street or by lamplight in Eclipse, but holding a conversation with him while he peered at her for extended periods was becoming a strain.

She was going to have to move on. Her regret put her in a grumpier mood than she should have been. After all, she still had Ned to cash in as soon as she figured out how to get him out of Deacon's clutches.

But Deacon wasn't having any of her rush. As soon as they rode into the McCallister barnyard, he let out a whoop that brought his brother out from the barn.

"Who's cooking this morning? Tell me Eden's in the kitchen and make me a happy man."

"Best cook in Texas told me there was a fresh batch of apple butter to slather on her pancakes and she was serving 'em with scrambled eggs, fried taters, gravy and ham." Sam grinned at Deacon and then peered at Miri thoughtfully. "Wondered when you two were going to get sensible and team up."

Sam's description of breakfast made Miri so hungry she had to keep her mouth shut to stop drool from spilling out. As it was, her stomach clenched and growled, embarrassing her with the noise. Deacon didn't waste time.

He dismounted and led Possum into the barn with Miri still mounted on his back. He threw her a brush, a bucket and a scoop and pointed her at the feed bin and water trough. She didn't appear to have much choice and the promise of a tasty meal tipped the scales, erasing good sense with hunger.

"Where's the counterfeiter?" Deacon talked to his cousin and his brother and she listened as she took care of Possum.

"Dan Hawks had use for him. I didn't. " Sam's tone didn't bode well for Ned Jackson. "I hauled him to Hawks Nest soon as you brought him here.

You'll have to question him there. I don't want the jackass around our women."

"Guess Ned couldn't keep his mouth shut here either." Deacon didn't seem perturbed by the change of venue for her prisoner. It made it that much harder for her to question him.

But the food smells superseded her impatience and she followed the McCallister men into the ranch kitchen for their morning meal.

"It's customary to take your hat off inside, pup," Deacon growled.

It was one of those infrequent moments when Miri's disguise got in the way of living. Here she was in the midst of a family get-together with people she'd really like to know and she was decked out in Beau's costume playing an uncouth Tennessee half-grown bumpkin.

Miri didn't know much about social etiquette and Beau knew even less. It was a good excuse not to take off her hat. The hat pretty much went with the wig and one without the other wasn't something she cared to risk.

"Pshaw, Deacon, quit picking on the boy. Eat." Eden moved Miri toward the kitchen table, scolding Deacon along the way. He still got to the table before her and made it a point to sit across from the chair where Eden seated her.

Miri scooted back some trying to make her lanky frame appear smaller and debating whether to leave or stay. The tantalizing scents coming from the kitchen were too much lure though, and she decided not to let Deacon run her off.

Since she didn't want to come across as a heathen, though she was one, Beau watched the others and tried her best to mimic their eating habits as she enjoyed the unusual inclusion in a family affair.

"How old are you, Beau?" Eden's puzzled look finally turned into what was on her mind.

Miri shrugged and deepened her drawl. "I don't rightly know my birthing day, but the folks at the Home said it looked like I might be pushin' three years or so when I turned up. I didn't speak none at the time and don't remember anything of before, 'cept it bein' real cold."

"You were abandoned?" Deacon peered closer at her and Miri squirmed some under his stare. It was tricky sometimes being two people at once. Beau's past was her past too, but...

"It was snowing real hard the night one of the teachers found me on the stoop and fetched me inside. She said I was wearin' a nappy and nothin' else." Miri had a vague memory of numbing cold that always accompanied feelings of fear. Though the incident had happened a lifetime before, goose bumps chased up and down her arms and she shivered in spite of the heat in the room.

"I stopped there nigh onto seven years. At first I waited for someone to choose me. But me bein' so big and funny-lookin', even when I was a young'un, nobody ever wanted me. In the summer of '71, a couple decided they was takin' me home. I didn't like the look of *them* and *I* decided they wasn't." Actually, after the man had cornered her alone and she'd stabbed him, Miri had decided leaving was best.

"So you were in an orphanage until you were ten?" Charlie's wife buttered a roll, her question casual but her look sharp. Miri shifted on her seat uneasily. Naomi had been a schoolmarm and hadn't lost the knack of getting answers.

"Yep," Miri mumbled. "The Tennessee Home for Foundlings and Orphans."

"How did you end up here?" Naomi asked.

"How did you survive?" Charlie Wolf's mother Rachel McCallister spoke up, adding her question to the other.

"I just crept out the night before I was to leave and kept goin'." Miri didn't really want to delve into all that but she'd roused the curiosity of the McCallister women so it seemed like she had to answer. Seeing Deacon's speculative look, she immersed herself in her Beauregard character, regaling the McCallisters with stories about her wild ride down the Big Sandy River on a log.

"I'da took the ferry like other folks, but I didn't have two pennies to rub together. So I made me a raft of sorts and away I went." She grinned when she told that story. "After I survived my trip down the river, I met some Indians and visited a spell afore I moved on. It was an adventure for sure."

"If you're an orphan with no people, where'd you get the name Beauregard?" Deacon asked. She figured if she didn't answer he'd find something else to query her about, so she told him.

"I never had a last name until a couple years back. I was choppin' wood in a place named Beauregard, Louisiana. I fancied the name so I decided I'd take it with me when I moved on. It's the longest I ever heard. I figured it fit me cause of my size, you know what I mean."

"McCallister is longer," Deacon said mildly, and then added, "there's nothing wrong with your size."

Since Deacon was seated directly across the table from her it was hard to avoid looking at him. The food was heavenly. Miri's flapjacks melted in her mouth as she forked in bites smothered in apple butter.

"You're a fine cook," she told Eden. "Might I have the recipe for your apple butter?"

Deacon choked on his coffee.

"What?"

"You cook?"

"No, but someday I might have an apple tree and if I do, then I'll have an apple butter recipe handy to use," she answered his startled question belligerently.

Eden copied the ingredients and instructions on a card while Miri and the men ate. Then she brought it to the table and laid it by Miri's plate. Deacon reached over, picked it up and read it.

Miri didn't say anything until he started to put it in his pocket.

"Hey." She reached across and grabbed the edge of the paper.

"Guess we'll have to fight for it," he growled.

"You think you can take me, preacher man?" She laughed out loud, taunting him. As a matter of fact, considering his recent theft of her prisoner, she was eager to put Deacon on his ass in the dust.

"Yep," he said grimly, staring at her.

It didn't take long for Sam to do his usual bet collecting and the next thing she knew, the two of them were in the McCallister ranch yard, ringed by the rest of the family.

Deacon took off his gun belt, handing it to Sam.

A prickle of unease coursed through Miri when the McCallister women lined up on her side and faced the men across the circle as though they were backing her in the coming fight.

I sure can't be losing now. Not that she was going to. Charlie drew a line in the dirt, stepped outside the circle and nodded.

"First one pins the other's shoulders, wins?" Deacon looked at her as he asked his question.

"Sure," she agreed. She had a move she'd been wanting to try out on someone and now was a good time. She pulled her hat on tighter and commenced to think like a Kiowa brave. Her opponent was bigger and brawnier than her so she'd have the advantage in speed. Besides, she figured he'd want

176

to keep his pants clean and wouldn't do more than take a swing or two at her.

"Let the best man win," she said, bouncing on her toes as she stuck her hand out to shake on it.

As soon as he took her hand, she ducked, pivoted into his hip and hooked her leg behind his knee, pulling him off balance and slamming him on his rump. Before he could recover, she fell down on top of him.

"I win," she crowed, grinning at the surrounding audience. "Beat ya, McCallister. Told ya not to mess…"

Her words trailed away as she gazed down at how she was straddling him and felt a blush crawl up her neck. She'd warmed considerably between her legs too and wondered if he could feel the heat where she was pressed against his belly. It was embarrassing. Instead of shoving his shoulders to the ground and pinning him, she scrambled up and backed away.

"Best two out of three," she mumbled, trying to look nonchalant.

"Absolutely," Deacon agreed, stood and stalked across the yard, stopping in front of her. Just like that, he wrapped her in a bear hug and said, "I've got you pinned. Admit it."

"No fair," she cried foul. Her arms *were* pinned — to her sides. She tried to butt her head against his but he solved that threat by lifting her off her feet and tossing her into the air. He caught her, holding her around the waist, aloft at least six inches and far enough from him to render her kicks ineffectual. He also wore a grin plastered over his face.

"Deacon," she yelled. "What in tarnation is wrong with you?"

"Gotcha," he answered, his grip tightening around her waist.

Gotcha? She'd said the same thing when she'd wrapped her legs around him in the Pleasure Dome's fancy bathtub. She stopped kicking, jarred from her Beau persona with a thud. Heat crept from her neck to her face.

Deacon winked and set her on the ground. Before she could run for the hills, he pulled her into his arms, molding her body to his. Shock waves rippled through her. She had a feeling she'd been suckered. She was acutely aware of his chest pressing against her unbound breasts under her buckskins.

"Not so mouthy now, are you, brat?" He was talking low so the others couldn't hear. "I like Calvin's wig better than Beauregard's."

"I don't know what yer talkin' about." She tried to bluff her way when she knew it was a fruitless cause.

"Don't you?" He put his hand on her rump, and in front of his kin and God Almighty, Deacon fit his long length tighter to her. She could feel his cock pressing against her mound. As a matter of fact, they lined up real nice.

"Charlie, I don't understand." Naomi murmured.

"You will shortly," Charlie answered. The conversation drifted to Miri, jarring her into action.

"Let me go. Your relatives are gettin' an eyeful."

"When I feel like it," he growled. Squinting at her and wearing a satisfied expression, Deacon looked way too pleased with himself.

"I'm in the middle of a hunt. This is not the time for shenanigans," she muttered.

"So *we* are," he agreed, continuing to hold her gaze as he included himself in her hunt. "Partners," he murmured, running his thumb along her lower lip.

"Maybe," she answered. It wasn't lost on Miri that he didn't ask her opinion.

It was hard to maintain the Beauregard persona because it was definitely Miri gawking at him as she stood with her moccasins fused to the dirt and he stepped back, releasing her.

Before he could say or do something else to fluster her, she turned away and headed for the barn. She didn't have to look to know Deacon was staring at her behind as she walked away. Her body tingled with awareness under the heat of his gaze.

"Better get saddled and ready to ride. Daylight's burning and Sam's already gone ahead to let the Hawks Nest riders know we'll be visiting the stronghold today."

His pragmatic words trailed behind her when she ducked into Possum's stall, making her wonder if she'd imagined the moments before.

She'd been pressing him to let her interview the counterfeiter, but suddenly Deacon was urging her to hurry up and making her feel like a slacker for slowing *him* down.

Ketchum bumped against her side, adding his opinion in the mix and indicating he also thought it was time to leave. She made short work of getting Possum ready to ride and joined the remaining

McCallister men, mounted and waiting for her in front of the barn.

The morning's playful expressions were gone. Miri straightened in the saddle, reining Possum toward Deacon's side. In the face of the grim trio, any exuberance on her part should have been quelled. The truth was, she had to force back the grin fighting to bust loose from her lips. She was riding with the McCallisters and it felt mighty fine.

As for his acting foolish in front of his kin, well, it seemed like the jig was up. He knew Beau was pretend, that Miri was the woman who'd come into an outlaw camp and saved him and gone into a brothel room to bed him. She had a lot to think about besides questioning Ned as they rode toward Hawks Nest ranch.

* * * * *

Deacon shifted in the saddle, riding his hard-on and trying not to stare at Beauregard's ass as he followed her horse in their single file trek through the Hawks Nest woods. In his quest to look elsewhere, he'd spotted more than one Hawks Nest shadow warrior. Renegade Apaches protected the Hawks cousins and their ranch. Nobody came on the spread without an invitation or an escort.

Having visited Grady Hawks in the past, Deacon was aware of the Indian ranch hands both perched in the trees above and pacing along parallel to the McCallisters, ready to shoot, knife or spear if need be.

Deacon wasn't surprised. Since Grady's father Henry Hawks had been ambushed and killed on his way home from Eclipse last year, the Hawks cousins kept their ranch well-guarded. Recently a consortium of Eastern bankers had been trying to influence Texas politics and gain valuable land. In an attempt to acquire Hawks Nest, they were currently claiming the mix-blood cousins were too Indian to own property. It was a messy situation that threatened to turn ugly real soon.

Deacon felt like a grizzly coming out of hibernation. It was clear from this new perspective that he'd spent the better part of the last ten years oblivious to anything but family business. Truth to tell, he hadn't been interested enough in his surroundings to care about what went on with his neighbors.

Now that Sam and Dan had become partners in the horse breeding business, Deacon's brother was invested in protecting Hawks Nest, which meant Deacon and Charlie were too.

That's the way it had always been for the McCallisters and that's the way it would always be. Charlie had rescued some female students when they were kidnapped from a young ladies academy. During the event he'd met and in his peculiar fashion wooed his wife, schoolteacher Naomi Parker. When they'd faced a mob because Charlie was half-Kiowa and Naomi was a white woman, Sam and Deacon had backed their cousin's play.

Deacon had performed a marriage ceremony and Charlie had claimed his bride. Deacon's gaze drifted over his cousin. Charlie Wolf was a changed man. The bitterness and hostility he'd radiated before Naomi was missing, swept away by the once-spinster schoolmarm who held his heart.

Deacon had barely adjusted to that family addition when Sam had fallen hard for Eden Pace. She'd been embroiled in a hunt for her husband's murderer. That didn't stop Sam from pursuing her or from dragging the McCallisters into an outlaw war that included the whole town of Eclipse and half the Texas Rangers in the state. Deacon had performed Sam and Eden's marriage ceremony too.

Now letting his eyes play over the horse and rider in front of him, he admitted the truth. He'd been envious. He wanted what his brother and cousin had. He wanted a woman who loved him. Beauregard didn't seem a likely prospect, but then again, she'd rescued him and bedded him. She must have some feelings for him.

The possibility that she didn't made his throat tighten. He didn't know what the hell she thought. She was mercurial, funny, endearing, brave. His heart kicked up to a faster beat as he admitted he had feelings for her.

No other woman fit the picture in his brain. She'd erased whatever tentative design he'd been working on. He wanted Miri and somehow he had to separate her from her disguise, convince her to trust him and then...

He swallowed, forcing impatience back into his cage of control. He didn't have to pursue her or claim her. She'd already done that. He thought over their past association meeting by meeting. At least half if not more had been initiated by her. And the Pleasure Dome encounter—he had no way to explain it away. She knew him and she'd chosen him to be her first lover.

Her only lover. Fierce determination to get this right flooded him. If he had to bide his time, he'd do it by her side. He didn't need to get to know her to make up his mind. He was already familiar with the brassy kid who knew no fear and the seductress who climbed in his bath and chose him to deflower her. Whoever she really was, she'd spent a year teasing his temper and protective instincts and now she'd roused his passion.

He wasn't foolish enough to think he could bully her into falling into his arms again. Well, hell. He hadn't bullied her the first time. She'd done the manipulating and maneuvering. He was surprised from his ponderings when Sam, riding from Hawks Nest to meet them before they arrived, appeared through the trees and dropped back next to Deacon.

"Dan's working the yahoo in the barn while he trains a mare in the paddock. We'll ride up to the bluff and watch from the overlook. But when we get close, no talking."

Then he raised his voice and said, "You hear that kid? Keep your questions until Dan says he's done for the day."

"Your brother needs to explain to you that Jackson's my prisoner." Miri twisted in the saddle to nod toward Deacon as she delivered her message.

"I don't see your rope on him." Sam flashed a smile that didn't reach his eyes. He had his back up and Deacon didn't know why. But he wasn't going to let Miri and Sam get in a pissing contest.

"We need him alive and we need to find the plates being used to print from. After that, he goes to jail. The thousand you and Dan lost to him will be paid out of my share of the reward. The longer it takes for us to question him, the longer it will be before we collect the bounty and move on."

Miri turned away from their conversation and Deacon followed her gaze to the woods on either side of the trail. Something besides Sam had her interest. Snarls suddenly emerged from the dense brush, signaling that Ketchum had found trouble.

He was surprised to see her unhook her whip from the leather thong holding it on her saddle. Carrying it, she slid from her mount and disappeared off the trail, shoving her way through the brush toward the sound. Deacon kept his rifle in his hand as he slid to the ground and followed her.

He'd been around Ketchum often enough to think of the animal more as a nuisance than a threat. But when they reached the spot where a fight was in progress, he knew his assessment had been wrong. The wolf was engaged in battle with an Indian ranch hand. There was no doubt that both combatants were going for the kill.

The Hawks Nest crew member had blanketed his arm and held a knife in his other hand. As

Deacon watched, he feinted toward Ketchum, taunting the wolf. Beside him, Miri reached for her gun. This was Hawks Nest ranch, they were the intruders, and aside from the fact that the fight was even as far as he could see, a gun would get them all killed.

She shrugged away from Deacon's touch but he took the coiled leather from her and flexed his wrist, unleashing the whip. Wrapping the fall around the rifle held by the Indian in the tree above, he separated the weapon from the Hawks Nest guard. The rifle clattered to the ground. Deacon flicked his wrist again and wrapped the coil around the Indian in the tree, jerking him from his perch to fall on the man below.

Miri entered the circle, knife out, making it clear she fought beside her wolf. Deacon was right beside her, his rifle up and aimed defensively. It was Charlie Wolf who slid in beside Deacon to defuse the situation. In a language the Indians understood but Deacon didn't, his cousin exchanged words with them. Then Miri joined the conversation, rolling out a guttural comment aimed at the first man.

"What's going on?" Sam called from the edge of the clearing.

187

"Beats the hell if I know," Deacon admitted. "But if push comes to shove, I'll take out those two in the trees over there." He spoke loud enough for the Hawks Nest guards to hear.

Sam nodded toward someone in his line of sight but spoke to Deacon. "Be a shame if I have to kill a couple of them too. Dan's not going to be happy about this."

"Not going to be any killing today." Charlie Wolf's words, spoken in English, were an order both sides recognized. The two Hawks Nest braves on the ground visibly relaxed as they untangled from the incongruous heap they'd fallen in.

But Miri, wearing a grim expression, watched Ketchum. It was clear to all that if the wolf decided to attack, she'd back his play. The beast curled its lip and snarled before disappearing into the brush. Only then did Miri sheathe her knife and walk past Deacon without a word.

He admitted to himself it was a damn shame when a man was jealous of a pet wolf. But as God was his witness, he wanted that loyalty for himself.

"Sure hope I don't have to go to war with the Hawks Nest crew over a damned wolf." Deacon knew that Sam's teasing remark hid two truths. He didn't want to mess with the business he had going with Dan Hawks but if it came to loyalty, he was backing Deacon and if that meant including Beauregard in the mix, then he was backing Beau.

"What did you say to cool things down?" Deacon asked Charlie.

"Told 'em we fight with the wolf."

"And Beauregard's words?"

Charlie Wolf snorted, an unexpected grin rearranging his usual stoic expression. "No way to directly translate but the gist of it was, *fight the wolf, you fight me.*"

"You've known all along she's female, haven't you?" Deacon remembered her tale about traveling with an Indian tribe. At the time, he'd assumed the story was part of the Beauregard disguise she used for the sake of distraction and entertainment. Now he looked at his cousin accusingly.

"Nope," Charlie denied the charge. "First glance at her in Abilene, she had me fooled. But when her pet wolf joined the fight, I knew."

"How?"

"I gave her the wolf when it was a pup," Charlie said and smiled as if remembering.

"You don't think you might have shared the information? And what in hell are you doing abetting a woman's danger?"

"She's not doing so bad on her own, Deak." Sam drawled.

Charlie shrugged and gave them a little history long overdue.

"I met her when she was travelin' with the Kiowa." Charlie's smile broadened into a grin as he openly savored the memory. "She was skinny as a rail, with white braids hanging halfway down her back. I don't know how old she was then. Like she said earlier, she was big for her age. But even though she was kicking every young buck's ass who tried to best her in a fight, she hadn't gone through a transition ceremony and didn't join the women in their purification lodge once a month. I think what she told Naomi earlier is the truth. I don't think she knows her age." He paused, his expression becoming troubled.

"The Indians said she just appeared one day and attached herself to them. They tried to run her off until she proved her worth, delivering gifts of furs she'd trapped and meat she'd killed.

"Even then, she was lithe, strong and she learned fast, mimicking her opponents' moves and besting 'em. She picked up their language fast too."

"Damn, Charlie. You don't wax eloquent about most folks. Sounds like you knew her pretty well. You were bride hunting back then. Why didn't you…" Sam stalled and frowned.

"She was a child, acknowledged so even by the warriors who waited for her to grow up." Charlie's information just added layers to Deacon's need to know.

"Well, what happened to her?" Deacon growled.

"Little Eagle had his mind set on claiming her as soon as she was old enough. I didn't think she'd take him up on his offer. Guess I was right."

Deacon grappled with yet another of Beauregard's hazardous adventures. Hell, she'd even survived living with the Indians for a time.

"So why didn't you tell me she was female?"

"Didn't see a reason," Charlie admitted. "You were doing fine keeping tabs on her, and if she wanted the world to know she's a woman, she'd wear skirts. Besides," he added slyly, "the way you two were going at it, you were sure to figure it out on your own — took you a spell to admit it, that's all."

Deacon felt like a fool. While he'd had his head blinders on, fighting the obvious attraction for a year, Charlie had been watching.

"And you?" he snarled at Sam.

"Thought you'd formed a tender for a man at first. Guess it made me look at the kid a little closer than usual." Sam reached for the wad of tobacco in his pocket, a sure sign he was uncomfortable since he didn't chew any longer. When he came up empty-handed he grimaced and admitted gruffly, "Hell of a lot easier handling the situation after I figured out that the *he* was a *she*."

"And you said nothing because — ?" Deacon growled.

"I had to catch my woman. You're on your own." Sam shrugged and grinned.

Deacon figured that kind of hell or high water support was something Miri had never experienced. He wanted her to understand that she had more than a wolf at her back now. She had the loyalty of the McCallisters. She had him.

But he was uneasily aware that Miri had evidently been making her own way most of her life. She earned a good living, she secured her own safety — she didn't need him.

From there he reached the next point. She'd seduced him, which meant that she'd wanted him. She'd trusted him enough to take him as a lover.

She used me. If the thought hadn't been so ludicrous, he would have recognized it as moral outrage. He'd planned to keep the relationship platonic as long as possible. But dammit, it wasn't more than hours since he'd made that decision and he was already conspiring to get his hands on her again. When they emerged from the trees to the trail, Miri was mounted on her pinto waiting.

"You had no call to jump in, but I thank you." Her cheeks were flushed when she handed him his reins with a scold. It was not his imagination when her hand trembled, brushing his before relinquishing the leathers.

"I'd better finish up my Hawks Nest business and get a move-on fast. Even so, I expect that Ketchum will come back after that Indian."

"Ever see him act that way before?" Deacon asked, trying to focus on her answer instead of the soft swell of her bottom lip.

"Nope. But if he tears out that Kiowa's throat, I won't stop him. Ketchum's a smart animal. We're friends by choice not have-to. He don't hate for no reason but he's got a hate on right now."

"Well, tell him to keep his hate to himself until we get the hell out of Indian country," Deacon said. He was pretty sure she meant that if the wolf killed the ranch hand it was because the ranch hand deserved it.

Miri took her whip back and coiled it while she gazed at him speculatively. "You got any more secrets you're keepin'? Why didn't you tell me you could handle a whip?" she demanded.

"How about you? You want to explain any more little details you might have forgotten to mention?" Deacon took the whip from her hand, waiting for her to answer him as he looped it over her saddle horn. No point in tying it down when they might need it again soon.

She had the grace to blush and change the subject. "By my count, we've got at least ten Hawks riders shadowing us to the ranch. Probably more now. No doubt each is close enough to take part in an altercation." She looked past Deacon at Charlie and Sam and grinned. "You think we can get on to questioning Ned before you McCallisters find more trouble?"

Chapter Eight

Miri was satisfied to see that the Hawks Nest crew had sense enough to heed Charlie Wolf's warning. The McCallisters weren't men to trifle with. The fact was the infamous trio had just backed her with no questions asked. That was something she'd not expected nor had any experience in handling.

Without a doubt, after today, Deacon's family all knew her secret. Part of her was relieved, though the reckoning would soon be at hand. She rehearsed ideas in her mind, trying to think of a nonchalant way to ease into the topic.

So, Deacon, when we coupled at the Pleasure Dome, what did you really think? Miri bit her inside cheek, trying to hold back nervous laughter.

195

She needed to pay attention to the job she was on, get to the counterfeiter, question him and find the plates. She also had the more immediate problem of Ketchum's feral determination to kill one of the Hawks Nest crew. But that didn't guide her thoughts away from carnal pleasure and into the proper channels.

So, Deacon, might you want to try that mattress dance again sometime? She carried on a one-sided discussion in her head as they traveled the path, climbing higher through the trees. She was acutely aware of the man following behind Possum on horseback, the weight of his gaze a heavy presence on her back.

Once they hit the clearing that housed the Hawks Nest stock barns, she set aside her worries. Charlie veered off to talk to Grady Hawks.

"He's got a Hereford bull I need to get to replace the one I lost to the bear. Grady might part with this young bull if I can make a good enough offer." Charlie's new venture in cattle breeding interested Miri.

In a way it made her feel uneasy. He'd left the security of catching criminals for the maybe of chasing good weather and wrongheaded cows. It seemed pretty dicey to her. Then again, he was married. Maybe that made a difference.

Sam led the way to an apple tree on the high slope overlooking the corral where Dan Hawks worked. They all dismounted and tethered their animals. Ketchum drifted to her side and stretched out on his belly on the ground.

She rested her hand in his fur, scratching him behind the ears as they both peered with interest at the horse whisperer below. Casually, Deacon sat down on her other side, his leg brushing her thigh when he shifted his position, getting comfortable.

Her face flushed, assaulted by memories that would not be tamped down. She wanted to turn toward him and rub her face against his chest. Ludicrous as the timing was and the fact that they had an audience, heat pooled in her lower regions anticipating another encounter with him.

Reluctantly, Miri focused on the clash of wills taking place below. The mare bared her teeth and flattened her ears, telegraphing her savage intent before racing toward the middle of the corral where Dan Hawks squatted. The Kiowa called him Dan Two-Horse—he looked white, dressed Indian and in the past had drifted through both worlds. Some claimed the appaloosa hunter and horse trainer was also a magician and said he *whispered* horses, stealing their will to resist his rule.

To Miri it didn't look as though Dan's magic was working today. The roan appaloosa plowed to a halt, spraying dust and dirt over the man, stopping less than two feet from the focus of her hatred. Dan crossed his arms and remained completely still as he crouched in the corral. The mare shifted her weight, stretching her neck with the supple elegance of a snake and opening her jaws ready to strike.

Miri tensed. Her elevated position gave her a balcony view of the corral and the solitary man using only his voice in the ongoing battle. He made a harsh sound in his Kiowa dialect. It was a rasping rebuke. The mare veered away, racing to the other side of the paddock, her tail in the air.

Dan Hawks stood and backed to the fence. The mare whirled and darted toward him, plowing into the wooden gate moments after he'd slammed and secured it.

"The mare's got him flummoxed," Sam said with disgust. "He can't sweet-talk her and she hates males in general, including the stud we planned to breed her to."

"Show's over." Deacon nodded at the barn and the man emerging with a wheelbarrow piled high with dirty straw.

"Yep. Ned's working off his debt," Sam explained. "He'll finish up his chores shortly. Then you can question him."

As a matter of fact, Ned looked different from their last encounter. Though he was hauling manure, he was a lot cleaner than when she'd left him in the Fort Worth jail. He finished his work, emptied the wheelbarrow and rested it against the side of the barn before walking to the horse trough to wash off.

Ned smiled at Dan Hawks agreeably and had Miri not known he was a liar, thief and scoundrel, she would have sworn he was Dan's good friend. She could tell by his movements that he was aware of his audience under the apple tree.

She'd tracked him all summer and knew that this was another part he was playing. Give Ned more than a moment's head start and he'd disappear and not be caught again. Then she remembered the blanket of Indian guards covering the ranch land between here and the edge of Hawks Nest. Ned wasn't going anywhere.

"You say he's Lydia's brother?" she murmured to Deacon.

"Yep."

"That's not a good character recommendation," she drawled.

"Nope."

"You think he knows where the plates are?"

"Yep."

"Is yep and nope all you can say, McCallister?" Miri turned and stared at Deacon, irritated at his terse answers. She should have kept her eyes fixed on Ned.

"Nope." Deacon turned his head, meeting her gaze, and it was clear to her Ned wasn't what was on his mind. She felt her color elevate again and with heat scorching her cheeks, she looked back at the counterfeiter.

"It was good of you to tell Sam that you'll cover his loss. We can split expenses before we divvy up," she muttered low for his ears alone. She risked no more peeks at him.

"Yep," he drawled. "That's what partners do."

His gruff tone made her belly clench. She didn't look at him again but she could feel the heat from his body touching hers with promise.

"W-we need to focus on finding these plates," she stammered, trying to sound like a professional bounty hunter and not a weak-kneed kid sweet on her first beau. It didn't work.

"I'm focused," he drawled, leaning close enough for her to feel his breath on her nape. She stifled a moan.

"McCallister, this could get real dicey if you don't behave." Her voice was steadier than her knees when she stood and walked down the slope toward the corral.

Ned watched her approach, recognition turning his agreeable smile to a scowl.

"You," he snarled, jamming the handkerchief he'd been drying his hands on into his pocket.

Miri didn't underestimate Ned's ability to fight. He wasn't tall but he was wiry and strong. Only the element of surprise had allowed her to take him prisoner the first time. She'd never get a second chance at him.

"Yer pretty good with them disguises," she drawled in her best Beauregard voice. She couldn't help but feel a curl of pride that a man who considered himself a master hadn't seen through her own masquerade.

"What gave me away?" he asked, his expression changing from belligerent to interested in a flash.

"Might have to hunt you again, so I'll keep that to myself," she answered.

Ned was standing by the fence, his back turned toward the mare in the paddock. Without warning, the animal raced from the other side, slamming into the wooden rails Ned leaned on. Had Miri not reached out and jerked him clear, he would have felt the lethal bite of the wild appaloosa's teeth.

He was noticeably shaken when Miri shoved him away from the paddock and toward Deacon coming down the slope.

"The way I see it, Ned, you've hurt a string of people who might like to have a word or two with you. I suspect I can find most of them if we ride back over the trail you followed this summer. I've got the time if that's what it takes to find the plates."

"You wouldn't hold me more than half a day," he snarled, challenging her to prove him wrong.

"Lucky for me, I don't have to see if that's true, because here you are." She grinned. Deacon stopped at her side.

"What the hell do you think you're up to, McCallister? You told Lyd I'd be in Eclipse, where there's a sheriff and rudiments of civilization—

things that my current accommodations are sorely lacking."

"Lydia seems to think she can get you off and out. I've got a pile of money invested in hunting you. I need to collect the bounty, Ned. So it's looks like I'm going to have to keep you secreted here away from Eclipse and civilization until the Texas Ranger arrives to take you to Fort Stockton." To Miri's way of thinking, Deacon's tone was almost apologetic as he explained to Ned why prison loomed before him.

Deliberately, she laughed, letting the sound of her scorn hit Ned in his pride. That was one part of him that he couldn't hide. Whether he was playing a banker, preacher or rancher, or right now a misunderstood criminal, Ned thought he was smarter than everyone else and it showed in the tilt of his chin, the set of his shoulders and the arrogance of his stride.

As one actor of sorts to another, Miri didn't think much of Ned's performance. He thought he could change his wig and that was all anyone saw. She knew better. Why, old folks walked one way, men swaggered and were bold, women minced, children... The list of differences grew in her mind.

"You're not very good at this business," she said. "You passin' bad paper so you can set yourself up in another line of work?"

The insult was more than Ned could handle. "You might have caught me, but you didn't get what you're after," he sneered.

"Yet," she drawled, correcting him. "I 'spect I will, you not bein' near as clever as ya think ya are."

Ned's features contorted in fury and he was ready to fight. He started toward her, his fists balled and ready to go a round or two regardless of Deacon standing next to her. Then Ketchum trotted to Miri's side and Ned plowed to a halt, his attention diverted to the wolf.

"Someday I'll kill that sonofabitch," Ned snarled.

"He affects some folks that away. He don't appear to take to you either," Miri drawled, petting Ketchum's shoulder as he stood bristled and ready to square off with the prisoner.

Ketchum was definitely in a touchy mood. Miri hadn't seen him like this since early days when they'd first come to know each other. The wolf's rumble turned into a full-throated growl and he bared his fangs at Jackson. Deacon took that moment to get Ned's attention.

"Ned, unless you've got some information for us, you're wasting our time. You can stay here a while longer and work off more of your debt." Deacon turned away from the man as if that was the end of things.

Miri took her lead from him and tugged on Ketchum's fur. "Come on, buddy." She tipped her hat to Ned and turned, talking to Deacon. It was pure bluff, but apparently it worked. They'd not moved more than a few steps when Ned stopped them.

"My freedom in exchange for the information."

"We'll come back to get you when you've worked off your debt here. I think we can find the plates without your help." Deacon brushed aside Ned's offer and took a step.

"Yer right," Miri agreed in Beauregard's drawl. "I tracked this polecat all summer. It'll take longer this way, but we'll collect on Ned and the plates. It's a better deal."

"Seems to me, everything starts and ends at the Pleasure Dome. Lydia might not be able to keep you out of jail this time, Ned. She might be on the court docket and sitting beside you in handcuffs," Deacon warned and pulled his hat down over his eyes.

"Leave Lydia out of this," Ned said gruffly. "She didn't know anything about it. I stumbled onto it myself. One of her customers cut me in on the deal. I'll tell you where the plates are. You retrieve them and leave Lydia out of it."

"Who's your partner?" Deacon asked.

"Not partner," Ned corrected. "Boss. I'm no more than one of his flunkies who just happens to know what he's into because I did a little detective work of my own."

"So why not tell all instead of one drib at a time?" Miri asked impatiently.

"I'm not a complete fool. After you get the plates and turn me in, I'll need something to bargain with when I'm dealing with the law."

He looked around and grimaced at the wheelbarrow against the barn wall. "Meanwhile, after due consideration, this place suits me better than Eclipse."

Ned appeared awfully agreeable. But tracking him again wasn't something she wanted to do. In her opinion, Ned was crooked as a dog's hind leg and had no sense of shame or remorse for those he'd wronged. Prison was a good place for him.

Miri doubted he'd even be prosecuted. He had one of those *trust me* faces people gravitated toward.

His expression was guileless and accommodating by turns. He didn't look like a thief or a criminal.

"And the plates are—?"

"Wrapped up in memories in the attic of the Pleasure Dome," Ned answered quickly.

"Time to be on our way," Deacon said and, as if on cue, Sam led their horses into the ranch yard and mounted his big appaloosa stud.

Miri climbed on Possum and rode between Sam and Deacon. Neither Charlie Wolf nor Ketchum was in sight. Miri worried about Ketchum's earlier behavior. But she was certain that wherever Ketchum was, Charlie wasn't far behind. He'd declared Ketchum part of the McCallister force. The Indians weren't to touch him or they'd have a fight on their hands with the bounty hunters. Unfortunately, Miri couldn't vouch for Ketchum's cooperation.

She'd be glad to get off Hawk's Nest land. On the ride in, until Ketchum's altercation, she hadn't paid much attention to the shadow riders watching them. But on their trip out of the ranch, it was different.

More than one Indian rider took the opportunity to break cover and show himself to them. At first, she thought it was a threat or warning. But then she began to get the awful sense that the men were, in some oblique fashion, introducing themselves to her.

She didn't mention it but when they rode through the gate at the Hawks Nest entrance, Sam drawled, "Guess you're going to have some competition, Deak. Better get your ponies lined up and your presents ready."

She knew she hadn't broken character on Hawks Nest ranch. She knew her disguise had been in place. But it seemed as though she might as well have a sign slapped on her head wearing "female" written in bold letters.

Charlie Wolf joined them with Ketchum loping along beside, waiting until they were distanced from the other ranch before he explained.

"You've got some admirers you beat when you were a kid. A couple of them are going to challenge you to fight 'em now that you're full grown."

"I've got no quarrel with them." Rats. She'd lived with a Kiowa tribe for more than a year when she was traveling. They'd been moving through Tennessee and Louisiana and she'd tagged along. Then, as now, she'd spent her time with the young bucks, not the women. She didn't want to fight any of them and said so.

"They don't want to fight you because they're mad. They figure if they can beat you in a match, you might consider them when you choose a *shikaa*." Miri gaped at Charlie when he said the Kiowa word for husband.

"She's already chosen," Deacon spoke up.

Miri opened her mouth to disagree, or at least add some words to the discussion since it was about her. But Deacon no sooner declared her taken than the three men surrounded her, herding her toward the MC3.

She might have been able to out-talk or out-maneuver one of them, but all of the McCallisters working together toward one goal was more than she could handle. She'd thought maybe she'd get a chance to say a few words privately to Deacon before she headed to Eclipse. It appeared he'd already made other plans—and her going to Eclipse wasn't part of them.

Then she dallied with the idea that they might get a chance to couple again before she left for town. That had her thighs clenching around the saddle and anticipation making her female juices flow. She didn't want to be unseemly but if she could have hurried the others along toward the ranch, she would have.

Deacon wasn't letting her out of his sight. Instead of the balm of reason he reached for, he pictured Miri facing the ring of Hawks Nest ranch hands with a knife in her hand. Then he reminded himself there were Kiowa ranch hands who intended to court her. He wanted to beat his chest and roar challenges at the Indian men who coveted *his* woman.

She's not yours yet. The practical yet sane part of his brain studied her ass as it shifted in the saddle in front of him. *She wants you.* The idea made his cock swell ever bigger and grind painfully against the unforgiving leather of the saddle seat.

Everything, including the counterfeiter business, was suspended until he solidified his claim. He was so filled with lust there wasn't any room in his chest for air. He pictured mounting her and had to stifle a groan.

The knowledge of other men who'd discovered Miri unleashed a primitive desire to drag her into a cave and barricade it so that no one could interfere with his mating. The stark reality was—he didn't have a cave. He had a bedroom on the second floor of the ranch house and five adults in rooms close enough to hear anything that went on within his walls.

He knew this because he had to listen to his brother and cousin coupling with their wives at night and pretend he was deaf at breakfast the next morning. Feverishly he tried to think of places he could take Miri. The old cabin he'd inherited from Annie sat on the other side of town and probably had spiders and jackrabbits living in it. He was humiliated by his lack. He didn't deserve to have a woman to care for.

From the front gate to the ranch yard was the shortest long ride he'd ever been on. He measured every step of the trip and yet had no memory of it at all. When they pulled up in front of the barn, Deacon still had no place to be alone with her.

It was decidedly awkward. Sam didn't bother to hide his grin as he dismounted and led his horse into the barn. Charlie was more helpful.

"Watch out for snakes." His cousin threw him a blanket before riding into the barn, leaving Deacon and Miri still mounted and facing each other. While he was struggling to find the right words to get from looking to fucking, she took matters into her hands.

"You got a place to unfurl that ground cloth, Deacon? I've a mind to get naked with you again."

If, want and *maybe* changed to *where* in a moment. Passion flared between them and it was all Deacon could do to keep from falling with her to the ground in a frenzy of passion. Looking at the blanket Charlie had thrown him, Deacon suddenly knew exactly where they could go.

His mouth was too dry to speak. He lifted her from her saddle and had her stationed in front of him on his lap before she finished gasping in surprise.

"Mind my animals for me," Miri called to Charlie as he reemerged from the barn. She was laughing like a fool and clinging to Deacon as he rode from the ranch yard carrying her in his arms. Evidently as needy as he was, Miri's long slender fingers nimbly unbuttoned his shirt.

Don't let me come across like a slavering animal. I've got to be easy with her. She's young, tender, innocent…

When she slid her hands up his chest, pressing her thumbs against his nipples, he groaned. When she touched her tongue against the right nub, he had to clamp his jaws shut to keep from howling like a beast.

She laughed, the low husky sound brushing across his senses like a mist of kerosene on flames. He jerked under the caress. He couldn't get through her top layers so he went straight for the gold. Shoving his hand into her buckskins, he breached her nether lips, his fingers greeted by her wet heat.

"Fuck easy," he growled.

She didn't pretend shy. She opened her legs for him and nipped her way up his torso until she was nibbling on his neck and clenching her channel around the finger he slid inside. As they splashed across the stream, she thrust upward and he gave her two fingers to squeeze.

He was little better than a crazed beast when he pulled up and dismounted, taking them both to the ground, him on top. She didn't protest, and the way she wrapped her legs around his waist, rocking against his cock indicated that she was ready for the ride he had planned.

He got the blanket laid and her buckskins past her rump but he didn't get her moccasins or his pants and boots off the first time. She was needy too. She made mewling noises of want and he opened the front of his pants, shoved her buckskins past her thighs and rolled her to her knees, thrusting into her from behind.

Deacon went from desperation to sublime pleasure in one motion as he sank into her wet heat. He followed her hip-swiveling dance, pumping into her as the walls of her channel massaged his cock. He grabbed her hat and pulled it off. She dragged the brown wig off as well.

She had a kerchief tied around her head. He shortened his thrusts, leaning over her back to nuzzle her neck and remove the handkerchief too. Once free, her hair cascaded damply around her shoulders. He wound his hand into the thick mane and pulled her head back and up, forcing her torso into an arch as he held her hips with his other hand and took her with jarring thrusts.

When he felt the coiling power of his orgasm building in his spine and tingling in his toes, he pulled out in time to spill his seed on her rump, relishing the way the white cream looked against the rosy flush of her round bottom.

"Uh, that was—"

"Openers," Deacon growled. He didn't know what she thought *it* had been. *It* wasn't over. He grabbed his shirttail and wiped his emissions from her rear.

Flipping her onto her back, he lifted her legs over his shoulders and buried his face between her thighs. She clenched and shuddered under each stroke of his tongue.

"Deacon," she gasped. "That's not right—"

"Right as God," he lifted his head and disagreed. Then he returned to heaven, centering his lips and sucking on the button of nerves at her apex.

Deacon didn't know the flavor of ambrosia but the taste couldn't be any more heavenly than the honey he licked from her folds. He savored her flesh, tonguing the inner shell of her cleft before sinking two fingers into her channel.

"Well, maybe it is," she moaned, arching her pelvis into the primitive caress as her orgasm pulsed. He replaced his fingers with his tongue, lapping up the new flood of emissions and pushing her into another release.

When she was pliant, satiated and lolling in his grip, he set her hips to the blanket and fit himself between her thighs.

"Deacon?" she panted, her look almost timid as he thrust into her.

"Don't make me stop," he groaned, slowing down and trying to grab control. He'd been in lust for Beauregard for a long time without admitting it. He needed this, needed her.

"I'm not telling you to quit," she answered, her tone cross. "But if'n you could see your way clear to smoothing the rocks out from under me, I'd be a lot happier."

Deacon rolled over, carrying her with him and letting her take top position. Her hair caught the last rays of the day's sun and glistened like spun silk hanging over her shoulders.

"Dear God, you're beautiful," he growled.

"Hush telling such tall stories. It's enough you want to couple with me." She pressed her fingers against his lips.

He nipped her fingers, then pulled her close to suckle her breast. She shivered under his wet caress and he attended the other nipple, recognizing the flush of red spreading on her chest as the precursor to another orgasm.

"Ride me, sweetheart. Let me see your pleasure when you come."

Her eyes sparkled and her hips swayed. She rotated her mound, grinding the lips of her sex against his groin and taking him deeper with each of her thrusts.

Her cunny clenched around his cock, stroking his flesh until Deacon also teetered on the precipice of release. Her husky laugh told him she knew his orgasm neared.

"Come with me," he ordered her.

"Bossy, aren't you, McCallister?" she asked, laughing down at him, and then went over the moon with him, screaming her pleasure at the end.

It was late afternoon when they'd crossed the stream. They didn't collapse on the blanket in each other's arms until the moon was high overhead. She was naked. So was he. Any snakes on the tiny slip of land forming an island must have fled under the assault of their passion.

Nothing but the sound of cicadas singing in the trees interrupted the night. She shivered and, remembering how she'd been chilled at the Pleasure Dome, he grabbed his shirt and pulled it across them, blanketing her with another layer of him.

He laughed self-consciously, aware of his cock rousing, already preparing for another foray although they'd fucked steadily since afternoon. "You ready to talk?" he asked.

"No." She buried her nose in his armpit, hiding her face from him. "Now if you was to ask me am I hungry, the answer would be different."

"Supper's long over," he told her, grinning as he got his sense back. He sat up, pulling her to a sitting position beside him. "I think my horse took off for parts unknown. We'll have to walk back to the house."

"Will your folks all be abed?" she asked, reaching for her clothes.

"Yep," he assured her. "Curled up and asleep, just as we'll be after I find us something to eat in the kitchen."

"I'm a sight. I need to get clean and I can't be going into your house halfway through the night. Maybe you can bring me out a plate of something before I head home."

"Where's home?"

"Well, as to that." She squirmed looking guilty. "I been using a little place that sits next to the river out east of Eclipse."

Heat prickles danced up Deacon's spine and stirred the hair on his neck. "It have a copse of cottonwood trees next to the water?"

"Yep. That's where I got my patch-up material. You know who owns the place?" She frowned at him. "I asked Hiram about it and he said it was abandoned and me staying there be all right."

"It sounds like you found Annie's house. Is it fit to live in?" Deacon asked, disbelief warring with a feeling of inevitability.

"It is since Possum, Ketchum and me put a roof on it."

Deacon snorted. "I have my doubts that as talented as your pets are, either of them can climb a ladder or nail a board."

"The two galoots I partner with aren't pets," she corrected him. "We're a team. I cut the logs but I didn't have a ladder. I had to stand on Possum's back just to get to the roof to rig a pulley system. When I was ready, I yelled 'hoist', and Ketchum and Possum pulled on their end of the rope. We did it. We got the logs to the top of the roof and I notched 'em and nailed 'em into the cabin walls. I told Hiram if the owner ever gets around to checking on the place, I've left it better than it was."

She squinted at him suspiciously. "You the owner?"

"It belonged to my wife, Annie. We lived there after we married." Though her living in Annie's house should have surprised him, it didn't. But her fixing a caved-in roof made his sense of protectiveness seem silly. Hell, she didn't need him.

219

She was an Amazon, a woman who didn't need anyone.

"Well, you should take better care of her things," Miri huffed. "Did you not love her?"

Deacon heard the censure in the question and struggled to share long-hidden thoughts of Annie.

"I think I buried most of what we were and what we might have been with her body." An unrealized barrier in his mind opened, flooding his brain with images of him and Annie when they'd lived in the river house.

"Yes," he said gruffly. "I loved her. I'm ashamed I neglected her property. I guess I didn't want to face the fact that she was dead and it was because of me."

"What happened?"

Haltingly he told Miri, letting himself remember for the first time in years.

"I was fresh from the seminary, first-time minister and newly married. I thought I was cock of the walk, preaching fire and brimstone in the pulpit every Sunday."

He stopped, appalled as he looked back at the magnitude of his stupidity.

"I don't imagine whatever happened was because of your preaching." Miri rubbed his shoulder and tried to reassure him.

"I wish that were true," he told her. "But had I not decided to pit my strength and influence against the scum in town, Annie'd still be alive." With the zeal of youth and stubborn need to win, he'd used the power of his pulpit to preach against the outlaws tainting the town.

"Ed Johnson wasn't my favorite sheriff back then but I went to him, asking him to stand up to the thugs who were terrorizing the business owners."

"Now I know that didn't work. There's good sheriffs and bad sheriffs and then there's Ed." Miri delivered her opinion using Beauregard's distinctive twang.

"One of my parishioner's daughters was accosted at the general store. Three of Dodge Henley's riders roughed her up and scared her to death. I would have been better off bracing the men myself. Instead, I preached against them, encouraging the church members to run the riffraff out of town. I should have kept my mouth shut and moved us to another town. I didn't and she paid for it."

221

Miri pulled his head down, laying it on her shoulder, petting his back and comforting him as he told her about how the thieves and murderers making up the underbelly of Abilene had conspired to rid themselves of the fiery minister. They'd lured Reverend McCallister from home with a false message from a member of the church.

"After the filthy animals raped Annie, they cut her throat and pinned a Bible to the floor next to her." His throat clogged with rage and unrelieved grief as he tried to steady his voice.

"Ed Johnson was a coward then same as now and it didn't matter that he was Abilene's sheriff and it was his job. He flat out said if he hunted Annie's killers he'd end up dead and he wouldn't do it. So Charlie, Sam and I tracked 'em down. And I executed 'em. It didn't bring Annie back and it didn't make me feel any better." He let out a gust of breath, heart-sick at his memories.

"But the heathens won't be hurtin' and killin' any more girls, so you did what you had to do. You brought the men to justice, Deacon." Miri planted a kiss on his forehead before reaching for her clothes. "You're a good man. I never doubted it. Now let's get back to the McCallister house so I can get back to my house, which is really your house, which makes me living there just plain strange."

Deacon stopped pulling on his denims, stepped out of them and picked her up, striding naked with her toward the water.

"What are you doing?" she protested. "I'm too heavy for you to be—"

"You said you wanted to get clean. So do I." He walked to the edge of the creek and into the fast-moving water that came midway to his thighs. It ran straight down from the mountains and was crystal clear and cold as ice. She made a splash when he dropped her. He returned to shore to fumble a bar of soap from his saddle bag before returning.

She was beautiful, mad as a she-wolf and shivering from the shock of the cold water. Remorselessly, he lathered his hands, gave her the soap and began scrubbing her body.

"You can do the same for me," he instructed her.

He winced when she rubbed the soap over his chest and pulled on the hair she found there.

"Ouch," he complained.

"Don't you *ouch* me, preacher man. This water's freezing." She washed him, he scrubbed her and

223

before they headed for shore, she sank under the surface, wetting her hair and reemerging to soap and lather it before rinsing again.

Then, paying him no heed, she stalked from the creek, shivering in the night air as she scurried to the blanket and her clothes.

"Use that cloth you wrap around your bosom to dry off. You won't be needing that again."

"And did you think no one will notice my big chest bouncing all over the place when I cash in my prisoners?" She paused in rubbing her hair dry to look at him quizzically, the jut of her jaw telling him she was prepared to tell him to go to hell.

He pulled a clean shirt from his saddlebag and dressed her in it, lifting her wet hair over the collar and buttoning it up to her neck. Then he smiled and ran his hands up her bare torso under the shirt, cupping her breasts in his hands.

"After we cash in Ned and collect on the plates let's try a different kind of client." He wasn't ready for this discussion but sometimes circumstances beat out good timing. He improvised quickly, deciding to approach their partnership as something that was a fact to be taken for granted.

"I can see that detective work is something you have a knack for. I'm thinking that there are plenty of government agencies that can use both of us."

Her belligerent stance relaxed into interest as she listened, looking pleased at what he suggested. Deacon had no idea if he could sell their services to the Pinkertons or join the army of undercover operatives the Texas Rangers had working in the state. He did know that he wasn't hitting the trail, sleeping on the ground, riding herd on petty thieves or chasing dangerous murderers any longer—and neither was she.

Chapter Nine

Miri hid her smile as Deacon planned her future. Aside from his high-handed assumption that his say-so was the last word on the subject, he had good ideas.

She'd thought more than once that it would be exciting to work for the Pinkertons. Landing a job with the Texas Rangers though seemed way out of her reach. But then again, Hiram's lawman friend Logan Doyle might be able to put in a good word for them. And Deacon seemed to think her dress-up skills would be something both agencies would want to employ. She was impatient to get on with their future endeavors and pointed out the obvious as she saw it.

"I think Ned has trouble telling the truth so there's no reason to think he did this time. We haven't found the plates yet, and he's hunkered down and comfortable on the Hawks ranch. We're no closer to closing this case than we were before we questioned him."

She was startled when Deacon disagreed. "I think he's telling the truth. You followed him all summer. He kept going back to the Pleasure Dome. Who knows how he got hold of the printing plates, but he's creative. I'm betting they're exactly where he said, in the attic."

She had a nagging feeling she'd missed something important. She tried to think back to the customers coming and going at the Pleasure Dome.

"The one I remember real well was Crispin. He visited on a regular basis but I don't know why. His carnal tastes ran in a different direction from most of the folks at the Pleasure Dome."

Deacon slid his arm around her shoulders and she planted a kiss on his lips just to make sure he understood that she could. He returned the kiss, caressing her bare rump with his hand as he penetrated her lips with his tongue.

Then he released her and stepped back with a laugh, grabbing up his pants and stepping into them before she could take him back to the blanket.

"Hungry, remember," he reminded her.

Miri gathered up her wig, her hat and the sheet of material she used to bind her breasts—all remnants of her Beau disguise.

"Took me a while to get Beau's character straight. Not to mention the fact that I've got lawmen who trust him to bring in the wanteds." She wasn't quite certain what he thought she was going to do with her life until they negotiated some new clients. But she knew. She had money to earn and outlaws to catch.

"I have responsibilities, Deacon," she told him. "I can't neglect my duties though it would be nice to have a breather now and then."

"What duties? Who are you responsible to?" He frowned at her.

She grimaced and shrugged. Best to get it out now so he didn't say she didn't warn him. Course, it wasn't warning but pride in her voice when she said, "I have children."

He blinked, his brow wrinkled. He buttoned his shirt slowly, watching her so intently she fidgeted. Then he asked, "How many?"

"Seven." She cleared her throat, surprised at how nervous she felt.

He didn't say anything. Miri finished lacing up her moccasins and stood. Deacon held out his hand.

"Ready?"

"Don't you want to know how I came to have seven young'uns?" His apparent disinterest peeved her.

"Well," he drawled, scooping her up in his arms before she knew what to expect. He was midway across the stream with her holding tight around his neck when he continued. "I figure there's a good story in it. I know you didn't birth one let alone seven. If you say they're yours, you must mean you're paying for 'em since I know you're not tending them."

She gaped at him as they reached the other side and he brushed his lips across hers before setting her on the ground.

"Did you think you were the only one who can figure?"

Miri blushed. Sometimes she was like Ned — a mite high in the instep thinking she was smarter than folks. She couldn't help it, because for the most part, she was. Guess Deacon was an exception to the rule in more than one way.

"Well, now that you know, you see how it is," she told him, shaking the wig and hat at him. "I can't just up and quit being Beauregard. I've got kids to feed."

"How long since you've sent money?" Deacon was nosey and seemed determined to ask the wrong questions.

"Why?" Her business was her business and she didn't feel right about telling it to him. Especially her money business.

"Because if you get your ass shot off going after outlaws or your throat cut challenging a pack of Indian braves to a fight, I don't want the kids left starving. So in case you decide to be a fool and end up dead, how much and where do I send?"

"Oh." How was that for a show of her smarts? It was all she could think to say. There was no laughter in his expression, no teasing as he turned her to face him.

"I'm pushing thirty-four and no prize. I was married once and my big mouth got my wife killed. I never thought I'd want to marry again, but I was wrong. I want to spend the rest of my days with you."

"I said we could be partners." She no more got that out than he had his answer ready.

"It doesn't work—us bounty hunting as partners—at least, not the way it's been. Times are changing. We need to change with them. I want you to marry me and go forward in a new business. We'll bring the children here. Naomi's been talking about setting up a schoolroom and this will give her more reason to do it."

Miri was stunned. He wasn't just managing her future now. He'd already commenced thinking about how to raise the kids. She was reminded of their earlier match. He'd just out-powered her. He was doing the same thing again.

"I'll have to give it some thought," she hedged. There were things about being married that didn't work for her. Like acting like a female. She didn't know how. It seemed pretty certain that Deacon expected his wife to look womanly. She didn't want to insert disagreement and disappointment into the fine time they'd just had, so she patted his arm and said, "We'll see."

He put his big paw over her hand, holding it to his arm and started up the path, leading her toward the house. It occurred to her that he'd not accepted her evasion.

"Deacon, I 'spect I'd better head on home. We'll have that food together some other time."

"No." His grip on her arm tightened. He looked at her and smiled. "We'll have it now."

In this particular instance there were some advantages to being bigger than Miri. He swept her along beside him, leading her toward the house, not breaking stride when she hesitated. He had a feeling that if they didn't get this straightened out and nailed down, things might never be right between them.

On the walk to the house, he sensed her growing uneasiness and when they entered the ranch yard, she veered toward the barn. They'd given each other pleasure and now she was ready to say good night and maybe goodbye. Hell no. He wasn't having any of it. He had a whole list of reasons for her to stay and none for her to leave.

"Did you not say you were hungry?" he asked. He guided her back toward the house.

"Deacon, you know darn well I don't want to go into that house. If any of your kin is still awake, they'll know what we've been up to."

"At least we spared them the noise," he growled, bringing a startled look of surprise to her face.

Her hair was damp but mostly dry as he gathered it up in his hands and bent his head to rub his face in it.

"What are you doing?" She tried to shy away from him but he nuzzled her neck, reducing her to giggles that ended in a moan of want. He also maneuvered them closer to the house while he teased her, blowing a raspberry on her neck and nipping her before he quit.

"I'm staking my claim, letting you know you're not getting away from me, showing you how much I want you and trying not to scare you away with how much this means to me." His kisses carried them to the front porch where he brushed his lips across hers with a quiet brush of assurance.

"If we're lucky, there are some leftovers from the supper Eden cooked. I don't suppose you can cook, can you?"

"Probably not any more than you can, Deacon," she answered. "Is it important?"

"Not at all," he answered, laughing. "We've got one in the family so far who can make a tasty meal. Aunt Rachel and Charlie's wife, Naomi, are still working on getting the hang of the kitchen."

"Does Charlie cook?" she asked. "Or Sam or you?" Her voice was tense, defensive. He laughed harder.

"If need be, I will. Or we can hire someone to cook for us."

"You're mighty generous with money not earned yet," she told him waspishly. "And if you don't let me get on with earning it, I for one am not going to be able to—"

"We're eating, then we'll set up a plan to go back to the Pleasure Dome and retrieve the plates. It sounds to me like with a little luck, we might be able to bring in the head of the counterfeiting gang if we want. Or just turn in Ned and the plates and we're a tidy sum richer with plenty of time to decide what's next."

Even as he said the words, he amazed himself. He'd dedicated all of his time and thoughts to hunting criminals for so long, he'd lost sight of anything else—until Miri Beauregard came into his life.

He had a moment of panic at the thought of losing her and ushered her up the steps and through the front door before she could think of a reason to object further.

"I'll see what's in the pantry." As soon as they entered the kitchen he handed her a sack of coffee beans and a grinder before disappearing through a second door,

Miri hadn't decided whether she was staying or going. The coffee beans reminded her though, of how good a hot mug of brew would be.

She capitulated to hunger, grinding the beans and lighting the stove to set the coffee kettle on to boil. Deacon came out of the little room carrying plates, eggs, a loaf of bread wrapped in cloth and a half-dozen potatoes.

"Looks like it's breakfast we're having," he grinned.

They worked as a team fixing the meal. By the time they'd peeled the potatoes and sliced them thin, the coffee was finished. Deacon poured two cups, handed her one and stood beside her, drinking his as she fried the sliced potatoes, browning them until they were crisp. She scooped them on a platter and watched as Deacon twirled the spatula in his hand and bowed.

"My specialty," he boasted. He turned to the stove, cracked a dozen eggs in the already hot skillet and expertly scrambled them.

Miri admitted to herself how comfortable she was standing side by side with Deacon, cooking together in the kitchen. Tenderness welled inside her as she watched him try so hard to please her.

"All right, let's talk," she said abruptly. "What gave me away?"

"You smell like a woman." He lifted the iron skillet and tipped the contents onto two plates.

She thought of the times he'd bent closer than natural toward her and the way he'd inhaled and said she smelled like Ketchum.

"I made it a point to stay clear of most folks, keep my tobacco at hand and make sure those I did business with weren't close enough to sniff me." She frowned at him defensively. "Most of 'em weren't, anyway."

"My turn," he said. "Why did you gift me with your maidenhead?"

Daggone she wished he'd let up on that question. She could feel her face getting warm and knew a blush stained it red.

None of your business, she mentally snarled but remained silent.

He set the plates on the table and guided her to her chair, seating her as he had the night at the

Pleasure Dome, as if she were a lady. That memory made her face get even hotter.

When he sat down, she stood and deliberately turned the chair around, straddling it, facing him and the table over the barrier of the back. It made eating awkward but she felt better with something between her and Deacon besides scrambled eggs.

"That's childish," he reproached her.

"Practical," she corrected. "I'm a tad more comfortable being myself than pretending to be a female."

"You *are* a woman," he said sharply.

She shrugged, marshaling her thoughts before she spoke.

"Eat your eggs before they get cold," he said gruffly.

"Did you leave God because your wife got killed or because you killed her murderers?" The question spilled from her lips, bringing a frown to his face. While he tried to figure out an answer for her indelicate question, she picked up her plate and enjoyed her eggs, feeling in control again.

"I didn't leave God," he answered quietly. "I left the church. I wasn't a good candidate for the ministry to begin with."

"Then why'd you go to school to be a preacher?" She'd wondered that more than once since, though in her opinion, Deacon was a good man, he didn't strike her as being a church man. There was a difference and she understood it though she couldn't have explained what the difference was.

"Jonas McCallister, my grandfather, was a tyrant. Anywhere I had a chance to go was an escape from him."

Miri listened as Deacon gave her a glimpse of his childhood, living here on this ranch with a half-crazed old man who used a whip to enforce his will. He'd decreed his grandson Robert's future, and Deacon had been more than willing to undertake religious training in order to escape the old man's cruelty.

"As for loss of faith? I guess most people—even my own family—think I rejected the hereafter when Annie was killed. Had it been possible, I probably would have."

She listened, fascinated as he explained himself for her. His pragmatic view of life was threaded together with an inner conviction that a greater power pulled the strings like a puppeteer playing with dolls. She shook her head at that.

239

"Nope, Deacon. I'd have to disagree with that idea. There's been no rhyme nor reason to my helter-skelter here and there. If there's a God up there managing things, he's not doing a very good job." She uttered her blasphemous thoughts, testing him to see what he'd say. "People claim the Indians are heathen, but what they believe makes as much sense to me as the other."

Deacon nodded instead of disagreeing. Listening to him, it became clear to Miri that having early been exposed to Charlie Wolf's Kiowa world of shamanism — a place where mystics, dreamwalkers and spirit guides prevailed — the young Robert McCallister's beliefs had been half-formed before he'd ever agreed to attend seminary and become a minister. Deacon's Christianity had cleaved to Charlie's Kiowa mysticism and developed something akin to what she believed when she gave it much thought.

"Call the divine what you want," he said, shrugging. "It doesn't much matter to me. I know there's a pattern to life and you and I were meant to meet."

"Whether by happenstance or decree, I've met some mighty fine people in my travels. I'm right pleased you were one of them, Deacon." Miri felt almost shy admitting even a portion of the feelings she had for him.

"I'm more than just one of them." He glowered at her. "We've been circling each other for over a year. I know what was on my mind. Before I even saw through your disguise, I wanted you. It scared me, I fought it, but I lost. And you? You had to have felt those sparks between us, same as me. I don't think all those stumbles across my trail were accidental. Were they?" He sipped his coffee, waiting for her response.

Miri didn't think it smart to confess she'd been craving a taste of him practically from the first time she'd laid eyes on him. She shrugged and muttered, "I had my reasons."

He thumbed his hat back on his forehead and gave her a shit-eating grin before he began ticking off possibilities.

"Let's see, hmmm, you decided I was the best bounty hunter around and you needed to watch a master at work."

Miri snorted at that one.

"You wanted the name of my tailor since you've grown fond of my shirts."

"Well, that might be the case. I'm partial to 'em for sure." An answering grin curved her lips as she looked down at her front where her nipples tented one of said shirts.

Deacon groaned.

"Now tell me—why did you disguise yourself as male and why finally choose me as your lover?"

His tone was implacable, willing her to explain what she didn't want to explain. He stood and walked to the stove, bringing the pot back to fill her cup again with coffee before topping off his own. "Tell me," he said.

"Well, Deacon. Think about it. I can't make a decent living as a female," she answered dryly. "As for why I had my way with you at the Pleasure Dome. Well, just once, I wanted to know what it felt like to be with a man and I figured me saving your life the way I did, you wouldn't mind so much being my first one." That was the truth, just not all of it.

"Your last one too, if I have my way," he said to her delight.

She loved the fierce possessive look he gave her when he said it too. It was something having a man such as Deacon wanting to be with her.

"Now aside from saving my life, any other reason for choosing me?" Deacon seemed real intent on treading into her thoughts where he wasn't invited.

She could have lied. She opened her mouth to tell a whopper in fact. But truth spilled from her lips instead. "I've feelings for you."

Deacon, being a strong man and quick to boot, lifted her up easily enough, setting her down to straddle his lap instead of the chair.

"I have feelings for you too," he whispered. "Hell, I had feelings for you when I thought you were a half-grown boy."

"Right, you had feelings you'd like to wring my neck," she said, rolling her eyes at him. He didn't laugh at her joke.

"Miri, if you care for me, I want you to let this thing between us happen. We'll work everything else out."

It was difficult to be irritated when this thing between them seemed to be growing. She giggled and hugged her mound against his hard-on and rubbed her breasts against his chest, feeling her nipples pebble through the material that separated them.

He bent his head and took her mouth, inserting his tongue and penetrating her lips. She was breathless when the kiss ended.

243

"I'm not a womanly woman." Which sounded pure stupid with her insides turned to jelly and his cock lodged against her feminine parts.

"You are what you are. I am what I am. Until death do us part," Deacon answered, saying powerful words that made her feel different the moment she heard them. Turnabout was fair play.

"You're an obstinate man and I'm a stubborn…" Miri paused, licking her swollen lips nervously. "I'm a stubborn woman. If we're partnering until we're dead, the way we fight that might not be so long from now. We both have strong ideas about which way to go."

"You can lead," he said immediately.

"Deacon, you think I don't know I'm being cozened. You'd no more follow my lead than—"

"What's your plan for getting back into the Pleasure Dome?" he interrupted her.

"Well, as to that…" Since she already had a good idea for getting back in and fetching the plates, she appreciated the fact that he knew her that well. She slid her arms around his neck and hugged him. "All right, until death do us part but make that a long time from now."

They shared washing the dishes and tidying the kitchen before he led her to a big chair in the front room. He retrieved a blanket from a chest in the corner and sat, pulling her onto his lap. His heart thumped under her ear as she rested her head on his chest. Every beat seemed a promise of forever to her. She turned her cheek and pressed her lips there, over his heart.

"Yes." Deacon sighed and closed his eyes, covering them with the blanket as they discussed finding the plates.

"We need to catch the head of the counterfeiting gang too."

"That would fetch a pretty penny, I bet," Miri murmured, half asleep.

"We've got seven kids to feed so you better hope it does," Deacon muttered and settled her closer, wrapping her in his heat.

* * * * *

Deacon woke with a start as the soft thud of horse hooves in the ranch yard brought him from contented sleep. Even scrunched in the chair with Miri draped over his lap, he'd slept better than he had in years.

He shook his head, trying to clear the cobwebs from his brain before he rose to investigate.

"Kind of early for company, isn't it?" Miri lifted her head, smiling sleepily up at him. It was Ketchum's snarl that brought her to her feet. She crossed to the window as Deacon strapped on his gun belt and picked up his hat.

"Not Deacon. It's you who has visitors," Charlie Wolf corrected her as he appeared from the kitchen, walked to the front door, opened it and stepped onto the porch.

Charlie addressed the two Hawks Nest riders politely in Kiowa. Deacon didn't have to understand the language to guess what was going on. Dan Hawks was one of the men. The other led a string of Indian ponies behind him.

Deacon wanted to grab Miri and keep her from walking through the door. Instead, he stepped aside and watched as she took her place next to Charlie Wolf. Deacon followed and stood on her other side.

"Dan says his ranch hand knows you. Little Eagle is offering these fine horses to us if we'll talk you into being his bride."

Charlie hadn't even finished speaking when Miri stepped off the porch and walked with purpose to inspect the ten horses.

"Mighty fine bloodstock he's offering, cousin," Charlie murmured in a dead serious tone.

Deacon watched as Miri lifted hooves, ran her hands down the horses' withers and checked their teeth.

Then she walked to her would-be suitor and said something Deacon couldn't understand. Charlie interpreted as she spoke.

"She says he's brought her many fine horses. She's honored that he thinks so highly of her but no thank you."

Miri handed the end of the rope back to the man who looked at Charlie and spoke rapidly.

"Doesn't want to accept her answer," Charlie muttered.

"Tell him she's my woman," Deacon said, anxious to get the man on his way.

Charlie delivered the message and Little Eagle asked Miri for confirmation. She looked at Deacon, then back at the Hawks Nest ranch hand and nodded.

In the blink of an eye, the man slid off his horse and stalked to where she stood. Deacon reached for his gun but Charlie grabbed his arm. "Watch."

Little Eagle drew a line in the dusty ranch yard with the toe of his moccasin. Deacon had good reason to remember that kind of contest. Instead of letting her fight the brave, Deacon strode from the porch and faced the man across the line.

"Stand with Charlie," he told her gruffly.

For once she gave him no argument. He mimicked Miri's trick from the previous day. Little Eagle wasn't expecting the move from a big, burly white man and Deacon sent him sprawling, then pinned his shoulders for good measure.

The Indian laughed unexpectedly as he climbed up and said her Indian name and then spoke in perfectly good English, "*Mahtaun Kheiye Tdaw Kxee* has chosen well. She is friend. Make certain you cherish her."

He turned, leapt onto the back of his horse, took up the lead line to his ponies and he and Dan Hawks turned to ride from the ranch yard. Naomi came outside carrying her Charlie's son, Wolf. Charlie took the baby, ruffling the curls bouncing on the baby's head. Before Deacon could ask for an interpretation of what he'd just heard, Charlie said, "Means Girl Warrior. The Kiowa valued her. She could have stayed with them."

"Exactly," Deacon said grimly. "But she didn't. She just—"

"Kept moving," Charlie finished for him. "I expect she had a reason." He added, "If you're going to mess in her life, you'd better be prepared for the outcome." Grinning, he held up his son as if to illustrate his point.

They were all too relaxed, paying no heed to Ketchum's low rumbled growl until a third rider, whooping and brandishing a feather-tipped war lance, raced his horse into the ranch lot. The wolf snarled and slavered, baring fangs and bristling in the middle of the yard. As the man completed a circle around him, the big wolf lunged and the Indian threw his spear, pinning Ketchum to the ground with the lance.

The Indian whirled, rearing his mount and whooping, celebrating his strike and calling an insult at them before he kicked his horse into a gallop again.

Above his head, Dan Hawks swung a bolo. The braided leather cord with a sack full of stones attached to the end sailed through the air and wrapped around the man's throat, breaking his neck. He toppled to the ground as his horse galloped on without him.

"Deacon," Miri yelled, paying no heed to anything but her wolf. Her face was blanched, her hands covered in red. "Help me."

Ketchum's blood spilled around the shaft but not at the rate it could if they removed the spear. The lance had knocked the beast on his side and gone through the thick part of his shoulder, coming out the other shoulder and burying itself into the dirt. He raised his head and whined, then licked Miri's hand.

"Slide your hands under when I hold him up," Deacon told her, grunting under the beast's weight. The wolf snarled and showed his fangs.

"Hush now, buddy. Deacon's helping."

"You get the blade from the ground and we'll cut off the knife end to let him lay flat when we move him." Ketchum's growl turned to a whine as Deacon lifted him.

Deacon cut the spear tip off on the one side of the wound and shortened the lance to no more than two inches on the entrance side.

"I've got to leave the shaft in. It'll staunch the flow of blood." They both knew that the wound would gush if he removed the lance before they got Ketchum to the doctor.

Grimly, Miri fashioned a bandage under the exit hole on Ketchum's side, all the time whispering encouragement. "You rest easy, partner. I've got you. You'll be good as new soon."

Little Eagle hoisted the dead Indian onto one of his horses, packing the body to Hawks Nest ranch with them. They covered ground fast. It was bumpy traveling that fast but if they didn't hurry, Ketchum would bleed out.

As it was, Deacon had no idea if they could save Miri's wolf but if it was possible, he figured Dan Hawks' resident medicine woman would be able to pull it off. She'd saved Deacon's life though she'd told him on one of her visits that he was a rare patient, being two-footed and human.

Dan and Grady Hawks owned a big piece of land and since Deacon wasn't certain where to look for the lady doctor's shingle, it was a good thing Dan was riding with them. As they entered the edge of Hawks Nest land, the wind kicked up and he could feel the temperature drop. He pulled his coat from behind his saddle and rode next to Miri to slide it over her shoulders.

They didn't follow the same trail they'd been on the day before. This time they climbed upward on a rough path through a thick pine forest. Deacon followed behind Miri who rode beside the travois. Dan Hawks drifted back to ride beside him.

"Little Eagle knew *Yuyutsu*. He says the man feared your woman's wolf. When I was gentling horses at Fort Stockton, he got in a fight with some soldiers. After they sent him away, he needed a place to work, so I hired him to ride fences for Hawks Nest."

Dan shook his head, regret clouding his features. "I didn't know the army used him as a dog beater."

Deacon frowned. He'd not heard that term before. "A what?"

"The white man chooses this way to deal with my kind," Dan murmured, his face settling into lines of contempt.

Since Dan's skin was as pale as Deacon's and his hair actually redder in color, it was interesting the way he spoke of the white world as something apart from him.

"The army paid *Yuyutsu* to train dogs to hate Indians. Cut a big stick, beat the pup every day until it grows big enough to associate the *stench* of our smell with the fear of the beating." He shrugged. "Simple way to produce an Indian killer. *Yuyutsu* tried to train a wolf pup that way once, but the wolf got hold of him before it got loose."

"Good to remember that the bad deeds a man commits have a way of coming around to bite him in the ass." Deacon looked from the dead Indian to

Ketchum on the travois. The wolf's ribs moved ever so slightly, confirming that he still lived.

"Yep," Dan agreed. Then he tilted his head back and looked at the sky, his nostrils flaring as if he was scenting the air. "Smell it? Going to snow."

Deacon inhaled the heavy scent of pine and maybe something else. "Kind of early for snow," he said.

"Not up here." Dan nudged his horse with a heel and rode farther up the line.

Watching him, Deacon realized that the appaloosa Dan rode was without saddle or bridle. The horse trainer was guiding it with his knees and hands.

One moment the land tilted at a severe incline, the next moment, Deacon's mount stepped up and onto a bare plateau. In the middle of the area sat a sizeable barn with a corral on either side. When they rode past, Deacon nodded at the building. "That the new birthing barn Sam's mentioned?"

Dan's grunt that could have been *yes* or *no* was his answer. Hawks led the way past the barn, his horse climbing the path pointing upward again.

"How the hell do you get up and down in winter?" Deacon shifted his weight in the stirrups to help his horse with the climb.

"We do." That was the kind of answer Deacon expected from Dan Hawks.

The man was an enigma. Though he had the features of his white father, a Scot who'd come to Texas Territory in 1849, Dan had spent most of his life with the Kiowa, his mother's people. Recently he'd moved back to Hawks Nest, partnering with Sam in the appaloosa business. Sam said breeding horses and the ranch were all Dan cared about.

Deacon thought about the doctor who'd patched him up after Beauregard saved his life. Grace had come to live here on Hawks Nest land and Dan suddenly had an urge to stay at home. Deacon didn't have to be a Pinkerton to see that the two things converged. If he hadn't been concerned with his own courting he'd have asked Hawks how went his.

Dan was an oddity who went unnoticed by whites, mostly because they only saw what they wanted to see — a pale-skinned man who wore his long red hair braided. In the past, he'd trained horses for the army and developed a reputation for turning out dependable mounts.

"It's strange watching him. He doesn't break 'em so much as out-stubborn 'em. He just sweet-talks them into giving up," Sam had drawled when

Deacon asked him about Dan Hawks' purported uncanny ability with horses.

The horses crested a second ridge and came out in front of a chicken coop. Deacon's mount snorted, prancing in fright as one of the hens flew in front of him. The horse pulling the travois shied sideways and the wolf whined, assuring Deacon that he was still alive. Miri beat them to the cabin and tied her pinto to a hitching post, walking back to the sled where Ketchum rode in misery.

"Bring the patient around to the side." Dan slid off his mount and slapped it on the rump. The appaloosa nuzzled him then trotted toward the slope leading to the barn.

Deacon grabbed one side of the travois, unhooking the sled from the traces. Miri carried the other side as Dan led them to a newly constructed section of building, hugging tight against the old. It wasn't fancy, but it was a nice-sized structure with plenty of windows for light.

"The doctor calls this her infirmary. She's treated cows, sheep, even foals. I don't think Dr. Souter has had a wolf to work on before." Dan's expression was grim as he led them through the door.

Wrapped in a voluminous apron, Grace Souter stood between a counter that held myriad medical devices and a long table that had hoists and pulleys above it.

He swept the room with a considered eye. In the corner hung a sling large enough to handle a full-grown cow or horse. Deacon's recent experience with her healing ability had shown that she knew how to treat human complaints. It appeared Dr. Grace handled animal husbandry with equal aplomb.

He and Dan carried Ketchum to the table, stretching the wolf out for inspection. Dan hovered on one side of the animal's head. When the beast halfheartedly growled at the doctor, Dan spoke softly to him in Kiowa.

"Ketchum knows his manners," Miri said, leaning close, petting the wolf's muzzle. As he listened to her steady stream of reassurances, cautions and stories aimed at Ketchum, Deacon was reminded of how she'd done the same to him on their trip from Pettigrew's camp.

Once, the doctor glanced up from working on the hole in the wolf's side to exchange looks with Dan. Deacon hadn't noticed the child sitting on a bench in the corner until Hawks crossed the room to stand by a copper-skinned boy of four or five intently following the operation.

Dan spoke softly to the boy. "William, would you like to help me feed the foals?"

Casting one last look at the operation, William held up both arms. Deacon watched with envy as Dan swung the boy up with a practiced move. Child and man both grunted in satisfaction. William clung to his perch as they headed for the barn.

"Need any help?" Deacon asked, turning his gaze back on Ketchum.

"No," the women answered together.

Needed or not, Deacon stepped behind Miri, keeping vigil with her and making it clear she wasn't alone.

Chapter Ten

Miri refused to leave Ketchum's side when the McCallisters moved him back to the MC3 to recuperate, so Deacon carried the wolf up to his bedroom, laying him on a pallet in the room, telling his female in-laws to shush when they had a fit.

Miri concentrated on nursing her wolf and let Deacon take charge of most everything else, glad to have someone watching her back while Ketchum healed. It was strange to her though, living in the same room with Deacon, even if he didn't do more than massage her shoulders or tug on a lock of her hair from time to time. She wasn't oblivious to the intimacies developing between them.

"I'd rather have a beer," she told him truthfully one evening when he brought her a glass of milk with a plate of Eden's food.

"Waste not, want not," he said, chugging the contents of the glass. A drop of white clung to his mustache when he finished.

"You need a bib," she scolded, climbing up from her spot on the floor to blot the excess from Deacon's face.

"I need *you*," he growled, kissing her forehead. "Eat first. I'll bring each of us a beer to drink before you stretch out and I take a turn watching the wolf."

He left her alone and Miri listened to the sound of Deacon's feet hitting the steps before she buried her face in Ketchum's fur. She didn't hug on her friend much anymore, now that both of them were full grown. But she'd been telling him her thoughts and her stories for years. It wasn't any different this time when it was him she was afraid she'd lose. She wrapped her arms around his neck, wiping away her tears and mumbling a prayer.

"God, you and me don't always see eye to eye on things. But I'm asking you to do this for me. Don't take him away from me. I know it's purely selfish on my part. He's a fine one and you'd be lucky to get him. But he's my partner. I'd take it kindly if you'd hold off a spell with any plans you have for Ketchum." She thought about her request and then amended it. "A long spell."

Gradually Miri became aware of another presence in the room though she had no idea when Deacon had entered. Pretty sure her face was a mess, she didn't turn to look at him. "If you were an outlaw, I'd be dead. I didn't hear you come up behind me."

"Ketchum heard me. He'd have torn my throat out if I meant you harm."

Startled, Miri looked down. Ketchum gazed at her out of clear eyes no longer dulled by fever and his tail thumped weakly against the floor.

"Charlie says he's only part wolf."

Deacon's words gave her time to get composed and she wiped her face on her sleeve before she answered. "I know that. After I raised him, I let him go. He tried to join a wolf pack but they ran him off. He came back to me torn up somethin' fierce. I took care of him, let him know he was welcome to stay with me. We've been fine since."

"You're both part of the McCallister clan now, and we guard our own." Deacon's answer warmed her heart. He handed her a glass of beer and took up his own for a toast.

"To Ketchum's recovery and our partnership." He lifted his mug and waited expectantly. She bumped her glass against his before drinking the warm frothy alcohol. It was just what she'd needed to ease the tension she'd been carrying.

She didn't drink often and when she had in the past, she'd been alone with Ketchum and Possum. She curled up on the bed and Deacon pulled a cover over her and took her place on the floor next to the wolf.

"Sleep," he ordered her. And she did until he nudged her awake the next morning. She blinked up at him and yawned.

"That felt fine," she admitted, stretching.

"Good. I'm on my way to town. Breakfast can be had in the kitchen if you're hungry. I figure Ketchum's well enough to sustain your absence while you eat."

Nobody in the ranch house seemed to think it was strange, her moving in, though they'd been a mite slow accepting her wolf. As for her being a woman pretending to be a man, the women just shrugged that away, talking *female speak* to her as if she was one of them and hadn't been pretending to be male most of her life.

"I'll be back from Eclipse by nightfall," he said. Since Ketchum was better and she was hungry, Miri walked with Deacon downstairs and went to the kitchen when he left for town.

The women were gathered around the stove listening intently to one of Eden's cooking lessons when Miri interrupted to announce her good news.

"Ketchum's doing fine. I guess he's too ornery to die."

She saw her mistake immediately. Three interested pairs of eyes turned to her. Eden set the skillet on the back of the stove. Naomi crossed to a curtained area, pulling the material back to show a tub. Charlie's mother, Rachel McCallister, carried a cauldron from the fireplace where water had been heating.

The McCallister women worked in a coordinated unit, herding her toward the bathing area.

"You poor girl, you're worn out. Whatever happens, you need to take this time to freshen up." Eden looked pointedly at Miri's shirt covered in rust-colored stains.

"I'd be grateful for a bucket of water, and that's the truth. It's been a while since I bathed." In fact she shivered remembering the cold dunking she'd endured at Deacon's hands. That had been her last connection to soap and water. She was a mess and it would feel good being clean. The women filled the tub, hustled her into the bathing area and left her to enjoy a soak.

She'd not ever had such flowery perfumed soap before. It reminded her of the rose-smelling scent she'd doused herself with in the outlaw camp. Only that had been sickly sweet, making her stomach churn a little. This smell was nicer. Miri sniffed the bar of soap, drawing in the pleasing aroma to remember later. Eden had advised her to pour some of the oil in the blue bottle into her water. She dribbled in the oil, then sank into a luxurious bath to relax.

I'll skip scrubbing my hair since drying it takes too much time. I need to get back to Ketchum. She soaped her chest, loving the feel of her breasts bobbing in the water. Miri grimaced at their size. She bound them most of the time. Unbound, she made shirts two sizes too big, just to get the material loose enough to hide them.

"Use that cream on the chair to make your hair nice and shiny." Naomi McCallister stuck her head around the curtain and caught Miri gawking at her breasts.

Miri scooted lower in the tub, concealing her body and her blush beneath the opaque soap film on the water. *Well I guess my hair's wet now.* She soaped it and rinsed it and then used Naomi's concoction as advised. Not lingering longer, she climbed out of the tub and wrapped the long pale strands in one towel and herself in another.

"Reckon you can pass me my clothes?" She poked her head through the curtain to get the ladies' attention.

"You'll have to make do with this, Miri." It was Naomi again, handing her a dress. "Your pants and shirt are too dirty to put back on."

"It's probably a mite short, Naomi, me being taller than you McCallister women." Miri frowned at the pale lavender garment handed in to her.

Naomi pushed the dress into her hands anyway.

"That's one of my sister's gowns. Comfort is a tall woman like you. Charlie went into town yesterday while you were in the sick room and brought you back some clothes for you to change into."

It occurred to Miri that the McCallisters had been doing a little too much thinking about her. Argument was silly since she was standing in a towel with water dripping down her back. "I'll make sure I take care of it."

She ducked behind the curtain and pulled on the assortment of clothing in the pile given to her. White undergarments with lacy trim made her snort. The corset she didn't even bother with. But she pulled the drawers on and the chemise

The dress was too nice to be lending out, and Miri wondered how Charlie had been able to coax it from Comfort Quince. She buttoned as many of the buttons as she could before stepping into it and pulling it up the rest of the way. It snugged some over her breasts, not hiding the size of them at all, and she wore a frown when she stepped around the curtain.

The conversation among the women stuttered to a halt and silence greeted her as all eyes looked at her with amazement.

"Is Deacon back?" she asked hopefully. His female relatives made her nervous when she faced them alone. Nobody answered as they continued to stare at her.

"I'll need someone to do up the buttons," she said self-consciously.

Deacon's aunt stepped behind Miri to oblige and as soon as the buttons were closed, the dress pulled even tighter across her chest.

Though she was grateful for the clean outfit, it seemed prudent to focus the McCallisters on what was important—Ketchum. She needed to get back to make sure he was faring all right. Her words were sharper than she intended when she spoke.

"I'll need my real clothes back. This dress is too tight." They remained silent, but Eden walked closer and tested the fabric on the shoulders.

"We can let the dress seams out a little right here. The waist needs a tuck or two, since Miri is so slender."

She stepped back, ignoring Miri as if she were a doll to be dressed and put aside. "The length is still a little too short. We'll let the hems down too on the others."

"I don't mean to be ungrateful, but I need some kind of a shawl to cover this dress before I can traipse around in public." Miri rubbed at her wet hair with the towel, trying to look commanding.

"Why?" Eden seemed puzzled.

"On me, this dress isn't decent," Miri answered sharply. She dipped her head, nodding silently at the fabric outlining the swell of her breasts. "I don't look right in such as this."

Nobody disagreed, a fact that disappointed her in some inexplicable way. Rachel handed her a white scarf to drape around her shoulders and Miri accepted it, wrapping it around her arms and across her chest. Then, being as polite as she could be, she proceeded to set them straight.

"I won't need the dresses Comfort sent. You don't need to fix them to fit me. My clothes will suit just fine once they're clean." It wasn't lost on Miri the way the women avoided meeting her gaze.

"I'll just sit on the porch out front until my hair dries," she told them and took the comb that Rachel handed her as she scooted out the door.

It's sure something, this ranch they call home. Miri sat in the porch swing and rocked herself back and forth while she combed out her hair. The bench was high enough from the porch floor to let her stretch out in comfort. She figured it was because the McCallister men were such long-legged fellows.

"Mighty flimsy stuff to be standin' 'tween me and the elements," she muttered, stroking the soft material of the borrowed dress as soon as the other women had left her alone. Nevertheless, she continued to touch the lavender material with calloused fingers, savoring the feel of what she had on.

She liked watching the people who lived on the ranch. They were an odd lot for sure. She'd been hesitant to mix with the women, having no experience in that direction. Deacon's introduction had been embarrassing.

"You've previously met Miss Beauregard in her male guise as Beau. She's a master of disguise, smart and brave and she saved my life. Miri, meet the family." Then he'd pronounced each name and though she'd met them all before, she met them all over again.

Deacon emphasized their partnership. Nobody questioned that they shared a bedroom. Of course, since she was nursing Ketchum, it was a moot point. She'd stood watch from a chair every night, sometimes stretching right out next to Ketchum on the pallet.

"A body could get used to smelling pretty like this. But I suspect it's wasted on outlaws." She sniffed her sleeve and grinned.

Miri grimaced at the long hair hanging stick straight down her back. It was so fine, it fell out of any braid she tried to secure it with. She usually wrapped it under a kerchief before she put on her wig and then her hat. She currently didn't know where her hat and the wig were, and that made her anxious.

"I need to get my costumes back together," she grumbled as she returned to the big open room they all lived in.

"Miri, I've never before seen silver hair on one so young." Eden McCallister reached out her hand and picked up one of the pale strands, staring at it as if mesmerized.

"It's a sight all right," Miri agreed, thanking Naomi for the use of the comb on her way through. "I keep it covered as best I can. It's unhandy in my business because it's something people always remember. I should have cut it years ago, but..." She shrugged, not ready to admit that it was her one female vanity.

"It's lovely. I can show you several styles that would accommodate the fine texture," Eden assured her.

"If it's your intent on making me into a passable-looking female, it's wasted time and effort." Miri frowned at Sam's wife. "I need to check on Ketchum. No sense in letting him get stupid and die."

When she entered Deacon's bedroom, Ketchum lifted his head and yawned. She crouched by him, scratching him behind his ear to reassure him that it was really her.

Evidently he had no difficulty identifying her. He closed his eyes and dozed, showing no interest in her female costume.

Miri held the hand mirror she found on Deacon's chest of drawers, trying to see herself in the tiny reflection. Her hair was shiny, hanging straight and long. She brushed her hand down its length. *That concoction Naomi gave me really made it soft.*

She twitched at the bodice of the dress, trying to make herself smaller or the material looser. Neither thing happened. *Maybe if I bind myself again.*

Ketchum raised his head, alerting her that while she'd been primping, Deacon had ridden in the ranch yard.

One thing for certain, she didn't feel ready to debut her new costume. Hastily she pulled the dress off. When Deacon came upstairs to join her, she'd changed into her spare set of buckskins. She hadn't had time to bind her breasts or put on her wig, but he didn't comment on her clothes or hair.

"Hiram's on his way out with Judge Conklin. They'll get here after supper tonight." He looked at her expectantly as if that news was supposed to mean something to her.

"And?" she asked.

"And, we're making our partnership official. I can't do it myself. It's not legal or I would."

"Exactly what is it that we're doing?"

"Conklin is marrying us. Hiram's introducing you to the judge as a friend and standing witness to the event." Deacon tried to school his expression to unconcerned, as though the occasion was of little importance. But she didn't miss his white-knuckled grip on the back of the chair, contradicting his nonchalant look.

When she remained silent, he continued with his plans and it was easy to see he'd been busy while gone.

"Ranger Doyle invited himself to the party too. He also wants a meeting with Beau, after which he says he's taking the prisoner to jail."

Miri leaned against the chest of drawers, drawling in Beau's best Tennessee twang, "It's not escaped my notice, McCallister, that you've fallen into making the big decisions and left the little ones for me to chew on."

She folded her arms, daring him to deny it. At her jibe, a smile curved his lips but he didn't disagree with her assessment.

"In case it slipped your mind, being Beauregard is how I make a living."

"*You* aren't Beau. He's a part you play and a lot of work has gone into that character. I agree there's no sense in throwing it away."

"So you're saying I'll keep using Beauregard when I need." The knot in Miri's stomach began to ease. Deacon crossed the room and stood in front of her, drawing her from her militant stance into his arms.

She knew there were other questions she should ask and things that needed to be discussed but it was hard focusing with him nibbling on her ear and nuzzling a spot on her neck.

"And then what did you plan?" Her words came out in a gasp as he slid his hands under her buckskin shirt and touched bare skin.

"After tonight, you'll be Miri McCallister and for all anyone around here knows, Beauregard moved on."

As she considered that possibility, hands that had been stroking upward stilled. Their heat hovered tantalizingly close to her unbound flesh, as if waiting for her response.

"Well," she heard the hesitance in her voice and wanted to slap herself. "I don't see why we have to get married. I like this part just fine." She stiffened her spine, coincidentally shifting his hands high enough to cup her breasts.

While they'd been talking and touching, he'd been walking them toward the closet. It wasn't any more than a curtain across an arched alcove.

"Deacon?" Her startled question came when he pulled her inside the tiny space.

"Trust me," he said. And before she could decide whether that was a good idea or not, he'd guided her to a spot behind the curtain.

"Oh yes." She sighed as rough calluses caressed her flesh. She couldn't see his face and maybe that was a good thing. She said in a rush, "You make me feel like a woman, Deacon. Like I'm the prettiest female ever put on earth."

"You are," he said gruffly, rotating his thumbs over her nipples as he spoke. "I want more than a swive or two before we go separate ways. I want you with me always."

Miri enjoyed his seduction but recognized it for what it was. "You think you can keep me senseless and get your own way, don't you?" She half laughed at the idea but since she felt dizzy with lust, the description fit.

Miri ached when Deacon abandoned her breasts, one hand sliding to her waist, the other pressing against her rump, moving her so that not so much as a feather could have fit between them.

"Folks get naked and fuck all the time. I want more than that. I want to be so deep inside of you that I'm part of your soul." He growled the words at her, the sound making her insides quiver in response. "I want to be part of your dreams and hopes. I trust you to hold my spirit in your hands and make me a better man. Hell, you already have. Believe in us, Miri."

Well there he went talking about spirits and souls, all the time herding her toward his own private corral. Miri was pretty damn sure heaven couldn't be any finer than Deacon's arms but regardless of that fact, she stepped away from him and out of the closet before she could change her mind.

"Whooee, it's mighty warm in here," she said, fanning her face and looking at Ketchum instead of Deacon. "I'm going to check on Possum," she muttered.

Lame excuse or not, it got her out of Deacon's bedroom and away from his gaze. She risked one glance at him before she went through the door, but couldn't really read his expression.

She avoided the McCallister women, hurrying from the house to the barn. Once there, she gathered her grooming equipment and entered Possum's stall.

"He says I hold his spirit in my hands. Daggone, Possum, that's a big order to tend."

Her horse snorted and stomped his foot as she brushed too hard across his flank.

"Sorry. This mating business has me flummoxed. I don't rightly see why things can't just stay this way for a spell. Heck, more likely than not, McCallister will get tired of partnering with me soon." But she didn't believe her own words and grinned shyly at Possum as she thought about Deacon.

"The Kiowa believe that a woman's role is to lead her man to the Great Spirit. Shoot, Deacon, being a preacher man and all, doesn't need me for that."

Miri's ruminations turned from resisting the role of womanhood to questioning whether she was the woman for Deacon. Nobody interrupted her as she carried on a one-sided discussion lasting the better part of the afternoon.

Deacon heard Miri before he saw her. She stomped up the steps, warning him that she was on her way. He loved her so much in that moment the very marrow of his bones ached to hold her. He'd been scared, afraid that the kid who'd fooled, terrorized and outthought outlaws would climb on her horse and ride away. Deacon looked ruefully at the wolf lolling on his pallet.

"Ketchum, if you've got any influence with her, I'd appreciate your vote of confidence," he murmured.

The ears of the wolf cocked forward and he gazed at Deacon as if weighing his worth.

"I'll protect her. Hell, I know you've done a damn good job. But you can't be everywhere she gets herself into trouble."

Wolf and man stared at each other for a moment before Miri opened the door. Then Ketchum's tail thumped on the floor in welcome. Deacon remained silent, waiting for the verdict. She stood by the door, arms crossed, glaring at him.

"We're going to have to do something about my female costumes. I can't run, kick or ride in the kind of skirts your female kin want me to wear."

"Our first investment," he promised.

"And you'll have to help me fetch the young'uns from Tennessee."

"Hiram's looking into it while we finish up the counterfeiting case."

She crossed to the chair and tugged on his arm, pulling him to his feet. "I don't know anything about being a female, let alone a wife," she whispered her real concern.

"I don't either. We'll figure it out together."

He slid his arms around her, took her mouth in a kiss and walked her backward into the closet much as he'd done earlier.

"What are we doing back in here?" she asked.

"More than we were going to do out there with your damn wolf spying on us," he growled. He massaged a breast, his fingers unerringly finding their way to her nipple. The nub stood stiffly, as if waiting for his attention.

She sucked in her breath when he took it between finger and thumb. He shoved his other hand under her waistband, cupping her sex as he waged a three-prong attack, penetrating her lips with his tongue.

His fingers ruffled the fine hair on her mound, tracing the line separating the petals of her womanhood. Liquid heat invited him to stroke and tease the soft flesh hidden inside the shell of her sex.

"Deacon," she moaned against his lips. He lifted his head and unexpected words spilled from his heart.

"Robert," he heard himself correct her. "I, Robert Austin McCallister, take you, Miri Beauregard to be my lawfully wedded wife in the holy estate of matrimony. I will protect you from this day forward whether we live in riches or poverty and whether you like it or not."

A snort greeted his words. He continued.

"I will honor your wishes as if they are my own. I will comfort you in times of despair." He pushed her pants to the floor as he said the words.

When her feet were clear, a situation she facilitated, he freed his cock and lifted her, temporarily interrupting his impromptu wedding ceremony as he seated himself in one thrust.

Deacon leaned Miri's shoulders against the wall, tilting her rump at an angle that would let him pleasure her nipples at the same time he thrust in and out of her sex. He regretted that it was dark in the closet when he pulled her shirt off because he wanted to see her breasts. He settled for tasting and set his lips on one stiff peak, sucking on the nub.

Her channel clenched and squeezed, tiny fingers of need massaging his shaft. Her orgasm pulsed through her, leaving them both trembling before he gasped out the rest of his pledge.

"I will love and cherish you in sickness and health, forsaking all others." He shifted his stance, thrusting long hard strokes in time to his final words. His seed spilled, filling her with his promise of tomorrow as surely as his words. "Until death do us part."

He slumped forward, leaning his forehead against the closet wall as he regained his senses. "Now you say it," he growled.

"Hmm, let's see if I heard this right," she said, teasing laughter accompanying her response.

Deacon couldn't see Miri's face but she kissed a spot on his jaw before beginning.

"I, Miracle Beauregard, take you, Robert Austin McCallister, better known as Deacon, to be my husband. I promise to be faithful to you and let you think you're boss along the way. I promise to work side by side with you so we don't find ourselves poor. I'm not promising to obey you because we both know that's not going to happen, but I promise to love you until death and after," Miri recited her own unique pledge.

He slid her legs from around his waist to over his arms, tilting her for long, slow thrusts. The dark closet and her wild response to his carnal hunger unleashed years of restraint. He couldn't roar his claim, lest he scare her away by the intensity. But everything in him screamed that he bind her to him with this taking.

Someplace between *I, Miracle* and *until death and after*, Miri stripped him of his clothes as well. His chest rubbed against her breasts, her nipples kissing his nubs as his tongue tangled with hers. She stroked his hair before settling her hands on his back, her fingertips digging into his shoulders as one orgasm rolled into another.

It seemed appropriate to him later they'd come to each other naked to exchange their first vows.

"Come with me," he growled as the lightning bursts of pleasure coalesced into a final crescendo of scalding heat racing from all points to one.

"Yes," she agreed, her hands coming back to cup his face. "Yes, yes, yes," she moaned, planting the word on each eye with a kiss before capturing his mouth with her lips. Her sheath squeezed his cock, drawing his seed into her womb and for a long moment they slumped in each other's arms, the power of their release leaving them both weak and dazed.

"I love you, wife," he murmured, leaning his forehead against hers. His words were greeted by a startled silence.

"I love you too, husband," she whispered and bumped her head against his to emphasize her vow.

After they reentered the bedroom, she huffed loudly.

"What is it?" he asked.

"You left your mark on my hair for sure."

He didn't bother hiding his smug grin as he looked at her damp locks.

"Guess it won't matter. I'm supposed to be Beau first, then Miri later, so my hair's going to get messed up under that wig anyway."

It was such a feminine comment, Deacon laughed out loud. She crossed her eyes at him and muttered, "I'll be lucky if I can remember what part I'm playing tonight." But Deacon didn't miss the sparkle of excitement in her eyes. "I'd do better if I had a female to mimic."

"What do you mean?"

"You know. Find a woman who does things right and make believe I'm them. I have to listen close, but after I get it in my head, I can darn near speak like anyone. "

Deacon considered the two McCallister wives, picturing Eden's sultry beauty and Naomi's prim smile. "Watch Charlie's wife in the front room and Eden in the kitchen," he suggested selfishly. "But you don't have to change a thing for me."

"Deacon, you don't seem to understand. I don't really have a real me."

"Sure you do. I fell in love with you. It doesn't matter what we show the rest of the world. But between you and me, Robert and Miracle McCallister, there's no pretense."

"Miri," she grumbled. "Don't call me Miracle. Switching from playing Beau to being a female is hard enough. I don't need to promise divine intervention with my name."

* * * * *

Hiram arrived first, with Logan Doyle by his side.

"Good to see you, Beauregard. How's the wolf?" Hiram didn't let on that he knew Miri was in disguise though Deacon assured her that the sheriff had known for months she'd been fooling him.

She figured a conversation with Hiram was in order but it would have to wait. Miri accompanied Deacon as he ushered the two lawmen to the ranch office. With Hiram confirming Ned's capture, the Texas Ranger agreed to pay the reward.

Though Miri felt she made a good case for it, Doyle balked at tripling said reward since they were delivering one man and not the three the law had been chasing. He did sign an affidavit guaranteeing them payment on Jackson though.

"Hard to believe a man can playact well enough to be three different characters and fool half the state."

"Yep," Deacon agreed, frowning at her smirk as he gave her credit. "Beau figured it out."

"I'll mention it to the powers that be. Might be some future work for you, son." Doyle barely glanced at Miri, directing most of the conversation toward Deacon.

"Best wishes on your marriage, McCallister. I'm sorry I can't stay to meet your bride. Sam's bringing

Jackson down to the crossroads and I'll take him in from there."

Hiram remained behind. Beauregard said his goodbyes and Miri retreated to change her clothes.

Eden, Rachel and Naomi were on hand to help her into the lavender dress again. This time, Naomi insisted she wear the appropriate undergarments. Miri obeyed, not wanting to hurt her feelings. It was nice of them since she'd been so churlish toward the idea earlier.

While they were poking and primping, she heard Judge Conklin arrive.

Sam knocked on the bedroom door and said everyone was ready downstairs. The women all left in a hurry and Miri trailed behind, entering the room in time to hear Conklin's complaints.

"I think it would be best if you moved that beast from the room." Red-faced and agitated, the judge didn't seem real partial to Ketchum. She could have told him it wouldn't do any good. The McCallisters were a hardheaded bunch. Deacon had said he wanted Ketchum as his best man, so they'd carried the recovering invalid downstairs to the front room.

"And who might this be?" Judge Conklin forgot about Ketchum and focused on Miri. He hurried to her, waiting to be introduced apparently.

"My intended, Miri Beauregard," Deacon told him, sounding as proud as could be. "You've met her kin, Beau Beauregard."

"Well, you're a mite better to look at than that young scamp," Judge Conklin said and beamed at her. "Where is he?"

"Beau's working and couldn't be here. That's why I'm doing the honors tonight. " Hiram stood protectively by Miri. After another swift look at her that left Miri wondering if the women had remembered to button her into her dress, Conklin agreed to continue.

Ketchum stayed. Maybe that's why the judge rattled off the ceremony sounding more as if he were presiding at an auction than a wedding. Miri was glad she and Deacon had made their vows earlier, though she held his gaze as the judge hurried through the words.

A smile tugged at her lips when Deacon winked at her and she knew he was remembering too.

"I now pronounce you man and wife," Conklin announced.

"Done," Deacon growled, pulling her into a bear hug that turned into a kiss. "Make us a good copy for our records and get that to the county seat

286

to register it," he ordered the judge when he came up for air.

The judge huffed a bit, but wasted no time gathering up his paperwork. Right before he stuck the documents in his vest pocket he paused and said, "Almost forgot. You both have to sign it."

Deacon watched Miri scribble her signature and then signed beside hers. Then he nodded at the judge. "Now you can go."

"Don't be silly, Robert," Miri scolded him in her best imitation of Naomi. "Eden has baked a cake for the occasion. Judge Conklin, won't you join us for coffee and dessert?"

She glided to his side, tilting her head in a manner she'd seen Eden use. "Shall we?" She took the judge's arm, leading him toward the door. Before he left the room, he patted Miri's arm and spoke to Deacon.

"McCallister, I guess I should congratulate you." Then he shook his head when he looked at Miri and blinked as though assuring himself of what he saw. "Mrs. McCallister, best wishes on your marriage. It's a pleasure welcoming a beautiful young lady such as yourself to Eclipse."

She inclined her head graciously, quietly closing the office door behind him before she spun around and drawled in her best Tennessee twang.

"Guess Naomi cinched the corset tight enough."

Chapter Eleven

Fort Worth, November 1885

Deacon watched from his vantage point on a roof facing the alley behind Rusk Street. His focused attention remained on the back door of the Pleasure Dome as he peered through the light drizzle. It was late afternoon and his stomach growled, protesting his hunger. The rain was almost welcome since hours before he'd emptied the canteen of water he'd sipped. He wet parched lips, hoping for good news at the end of this day's vigil. The back door opened and the sound of footsteps echoed hollowly in the otherwise heavy silence blanketing the alley.

The three cleaning women were uniform in appearance, each hunching under a wool shawl pulled high, protecting her head from rain. Two of

289

the three old ladies carried on a heated conversation that Deacon strained to hear.

"The waste in the kitchen, 'tis a sin, I tell ye."

"'Tis crumbs from the table of sin we use to bake the bread we eat. Hush now."

The third woman limped quietly beside them as they picked their way through rubble and refuse littering the rough path behind the brothel.

"Sin or no, I'll not be spending another day working for that demon woman." The sound of the Irish lilt carried surprisingly well for an old woman. Deacon tensed. *She's found them.*

"Ye'll be here tomorrow same as Callie and me," the other woman scoffed. "Better wear a thicker shawl tomorrow, dearie. It's that cold out here."

Deacon agreed, flexing his hands. His fingers were stiff inside his leather gloves and the dress coat he wore over his suit had ceased shedding water hours before.

The old women disappeared from sight, leaving him alone but for the rats scurrying from building to building. He crawled across the slippery roof and lowered himself to the ground, eager to wrap up this case.

Not trusting anyone, including the government agents and Pinkerton detectives, he and Miri had arrived in Fort Worth and rented a suite of rooms at the Ellis Hotel across town. Deacon had let it be known when they'd checked in that he and Miri were honeymooning and would be leaving early each day for social visits and shopping. When they were in, they wanted to be left alone.

Miri had worked in the Pleasure Dome long enough to know the cleaning service schedule. Nobody questioned the stooped and gnarled Irishwoman who appeared for work at the brothel one morning when the regular maids entered.

She'd cleaned her assigned rooms while she waited for an opportunity to search the attic. It had taken her three days, arriving at dawn and leaving at dusk while Deacon remained on his roof perch, prepared to go in with guns blazing if she missed one of their arranged hourly signals.

"We felt the ground shake when you fell, brother. The woman's got you tied up in knots and you're not escaping," Sam had teased him about being besotted. Deacon figured that was as good a description as any.

He planned on keeping Miri safe and happy. To that goal, Deacon kept his mouth shut, didn't talk about how he felt and didn't make the mistake of trying to corral her high spirits. He understood his role as her protector and guide. He accepted that she saw him as a friend and partner and told himself he was a lucky man.

He hadn't quarreled after the wedding with her plan to retrieve the plates. He'd watched her assemble her cleaning lady costume, admired her performance when she auditioned the disguise for him, and they'd left immediately for Fort Worth.

Once they'd checked in to the Ellis Hotel, they set the plan in motion. Deacon knew without doubt that Lydia's guards would be merciless to any man or woman they caught snooping in the brothel's attic. From the moment Miri went in each morning with the cleaning crew to the afternoon when she emerged from the Pleasure Dome, he died a thousand deaths.

From her oblique message, it appeared his vigil had ended. Instead of following the cleaning women, Deacon lowered himself to the ground, cut through the alley and hurried to the street in front of the building. Once there, he strolled down the sidewalk, greeting the fashionable woman waiting for him.

"Did you complete your shopping?" he asked.

"Most certainly," she assured him in the sweet Southern drawl he'd now come to recognize as her real voice.

Her shawl, no longer covering her head, had been turned into an elegant cape fitting over her shoulders. With her skirts let down and a hat pinned above the twist of silver hair at her nape, no one would have recognized the woman who emerged from the alley as the old lady who'd entered the other end.

"You need a heavier coat." Miri tilted her head, scolding him as she brushed beads of ice from his jacket sleeve. Under cover of her fussing, her words were pure business. "The plates were wrapped in an oilskin pouch and hidden in a trunk under a stack of paintings."

Using a slippery spot on the walkway as an excuse, he put his hand on Miri's back, smoothing the fabric of the cape. He grunted, feeling the extra bulk that signified the plates were inside the hidden pouches.

Once back in the room, she slipped off the outerwear, unpinned the fancy hat, set it aside and curtsied. Then the imp looked at him from sly eyes and said, "I'm fixin' to have my way with you,

McCallister, so if'n you've got somethin' to say that needs tellin', best spit it out quick."

Miri crossed the floor to where he stood, stopping in front of him and frowning at the damp condition of his coat as she removed it. Then she pulled his shirt from his waistband. Her hands were warm and he shivered, not realizing until her heated flesh caressed his bare chest how chilled he was.

"I knew you had to be freezing up on that roof," she said grimly. "What is it about *catching pneumonia* that you don't understand?" She continued the argument they'd started before dawn. When she'd felt the cold temperature of morning, she'd decided she'd be fine alone. He'd disagreed.

"You can make it up to me," he grinned, enjoying the way she pet him, playing in the hair on his chest before teasing his nipples.

"I intend to do just that," she murmured as she shifted her attention to his buttons. In a moment, she'd divested him of his shirt and had his suit pants undone, ready to remove.

"I need to take my boots off first," he said mildly.

"Then sit on the bed and I'll put them off," she ordered him. Her expression remained serious.

"What's got your tail in a twist?" he asked, staring down at the top of her head as she pulled off his footgear then went to work on his pants and the long johns he'd worn underneath.

"Soak," she ordered him. While he'd been disrobing, a tub of water she'd had prepared steamed across the room. He half expected her to climb into the bath with him but she didn't. As good as the hot bath felt, the bed was more inviting. He finished quickly, accepting the drying cloth she handed him when he stepped from the water.

In moments, he lost the towel and slid between the sheets, stark naked and tucked under blankets she pulled up to his chin. "You climbing under these covers with me?" he asked, catching her hand and tugging on it.

"Soon as I finish getting you cosseted, I'll be having my own bath. Then you can have your cuddling."

Her cosseting included a cup of tea and honey he accepted after she added a generous dollop of whiskey. Miri's rough-and-tumble manners coupled with her artless innocence aroused both passionate and tender feelings. He sat in the bed, sipping the hot drink and watching her.

"You don't seem to mind me gawking at you," she glowered at him. "Me, I don't cotton to it." With those words, she pulled the screen in front of the tub.

"Let the cuddling commence," he murmured, setting the empty cup on the saucer before crossing his arms on the pillow behind his head. He didn't explain to her that the opaque screen provided a sensual show.

He watched her shadowed silhouette disrobe and step into the bath. He stifled his groan, listening to the splash as she slid into the bath, imagining the rivulets of water running down her body.

By the time she stepped back into his sight, his cock tented the sheets and that was before he saw her costume. She'd donned a familiar ruffled shirt and wore it half buttoned over nothing else. Pale hair framed her exotic eyes before becoming a cascade of silver down her back.

"Since this is our true honeymoon, McCallister," she said, "I've things to tell you, so listen up." The real Miri, stripped of all artifice and disguise, approached the bed.

She folded her arms, pulling the material taut over her turgid peaks. Deacon swallowed his lust and tried to pay attention to her words.

"I might be a wanted woman. I think I killed a man back in Tennessee. I've been moving ever since. I should have told you before I let you tie us together."

"So you're not an orphan?" he asked carefully.

"What I said about being in the Tennessee Home for Foundlings and Orphans is all true. And me leaving when I was around ten, that's true too. I just didn't mention that I left a body behind." She frowned at him and waited expectantly.

Deacon remained silent, recalling her Thanksgiving tale of adventure and wild rides. Then he reached out and took her hand, pulling her under the sheet with him.

"The husband in the couple who wanted to take you home?"

"Yep." Her clipped answer resounded of Beauregard, the tough kid, the male stripling who'd thrash anyone in a fair fight. But the illusion was dispelled when she trembled in his arms.

"Tell me," Deacon growled, hugging her close.

"He decided I was going to kiss his man parts and I decided I wasn't." Beneath Beauregard's nonchalant drawl, Deacon heard the remnants of outrage.

"And?" He tipped her chin so that she met his gaze.

"I stabbed him with a pair of scissors." Her response was brusque and unrepentant.

"Did you check the body to make sure he was dead?" Deacon asked.

"No, I ran like hell. But if he wasn't dead, it wasn't because I didn't try to kill him." Miri looked at him from eyes shadowed with guilt and regret. "I just thought you should know."

"And that was ten years ago?" Deacon asked.

"Closer to eleven," she admitted. "You might say my own crime led me into my career. It was handy having an excuse to look at wanted posters, though the older I got, the less I worried."

"You can quit worrying," Deacon assured her. "Hiram checked with the Tennessee lawmen he knows. There's no reward offered for a young woman of your description."

"Being Beauregard most of my life, I just hoped folks forgot about me." Then she thought about his words and tilted her head sideways, more curious than alarmed. "Hiram asked after me?"

"Yep. He considers you a good friend and worried that you were hiding from the law. He checked. But there's no record of an unresolved murder of a Tennessee man killed by a young girl," he assured her. "If the bastard's dead, nobody cared."

She was still frowning. Apparently his declaration of her innocence didn't alleviate what was on her mind.

She sat next to him, peering down at his face. "You want to undo our partnership now that you know maybe I'm a murderess?"

"You didn't commit murder. Worst-case scenario, you killed in self-defense, though it sounds more like you should have received a bounty on his ugly hide." He cupped her chin and ran his thumb across her bottom lip, studying her as he explained. "Let me assure you, if you left him dead, I don't care. He deserved what he got and whatever you did doesn't change things between us."

"Be that as it may, I've a mind to keep things honest between us." Miri relaxed, tension easing from her shoulders as if she'd actually believed he might repudiate her.

"I think we've always dealt with each other honestly," he protested.

"Businesswise I've no worries about pulling my own weight in this partnership. It's the bedroom stuff I'm trying to sort out." She stared at him, her expression grim.

"Have I done something to frighten you?" he asked quickly.

"You set your mouth on my private parts," she answered, her face turning rosy pink.

"I'll never do it again if you didn't enjoy it." Deacon was swamped with regret for forgetting about her innocence and introducing her to his carnal hunger.

"You pleasured me fine that way. Can't be denying you the same, though I want to let you know up front, I don't expect to like kissing you down there."

"You don't need to do that," he said gruffly through stiff lips.

"We're partners. I'll be tasting you now, the same as you tasted me." She chewed her bottom lip and stared at the sheet covering his groin as if it hid a nest of snakes.

Deacon remained completely still. His erection had subsided during the conversation. But when she declared her intent to sample his cock, it ceased behaving with polite regard for her anxiety, standing tall in delighted anticipation.

Without further hesitation, she ducked under the sheet, sequestering herself with the object of her interest.

"It's too dadblamed dark in here. I can't really see," she complained, gripping his flesh in her hand.

"Not a problem," he answered, eager to assist. In a moment, he had the bedclothes thrown aside and she knelt beside him, clasping his shaft in her hand, conducting her inspection.

Deacon tensed, rigid under the touch turning his hard length to molten stone as Miri traced the creamy fluid leaking from his cock head.

Still not meeting his gaze, she wet her lips, looked at her moist finger, paused, then unexpectedly leaned down and licked the cream from his slit.

Grabbing the sheet on either side of him, he anchored himself, straining to maintain control, but he couldn't stop his jerk of surprise.

"Did I do something wrong?" she asked as she pet his shaft anxiously.

"Tickled," he groaned. Actually a jolt of heat had shot straight to his balls, but he didn't waste time describing the indescribable.

301

"I like the way this feels," she murmured, stroking her hand up and down his cock. He did too.

"You sure you want to do this?" he was compelled to ask. When she nodded affirmative, he added, "Grip it tighter." Deacon figured if she wanted to learn, he might as well explain the particulars so they'd both be satisfied.

He leaned back on the pillow, cupping her breast and kneading her silken flesh. As he watched her hover indecisively above the head of his cock he thumbed her nipple absently. Her moaned response made him smile. He pulled her higher so that her long body lay tight against his.

"Just let me kiss you," he told her. "Holding you in my arms with your lips on mine is enough heaven for any man."

He cupped the back of her head and covered her mouth with his. She opened for him, returning the touch of his tongue with her own. Deacon caressed her hair, deepening the kiss until they breathed as one. When he lifted his head, her eyes were heavy with desire.

"I love you," he murmured, meeting her molten gaze. "And I don't ever want you to do anything with me you don't want to do." Then he thought about her standing in the middle of the street, blasting away at outlaws and amended it to, "In the bedroom, that is. Out on the trail, whether you want to or not, you listen to me."

"I love you too, Deacon McCallister. Even if you are bossy," she whispered, staring at him fiercely. "And you can't be getting shot, or stabbed or *catching pneumonia* out of stubborn dumbness." She crossed her eyes and wrinkled her nose playfully, bringing him back to her original complaint, easing the moment with laughter as she stared at him with desire.

Abruptly she sat up, and, before he realized her intent, leaned over him and swiped her tongue across the head of his cock.

"Maybe it's an acquired taste," she conceded. "I'll have to sample it some before I decide yay or nay."

Deacon tried to hold on to his sanity this time as she tasted, licking up the side of his hard length and stopping to wiggle her tongue in his slit. He groaned in pleasure when her tongue danced over his rigid flesh before she took more of his arousal in her mouth.

"Good?" she asked, mumbling around his flesh as she met his gaze. The tentative movement of her lips brought his hips off the bed and he could only nod incoherently.

She sucked harder, taking him deeper. He remained still, holding back his need to fill the hot cavern of her mouth. But she bobbed her head up and down, taking more of his cock each time and sucking harder with each of her own thrusts.

After he'd suffered the ecstasy of her attentions to the breaking point, when even his toes were curled in his effort to hold back his orgasm, he rolled her onto her back.

"Now," he growled, "my turn." Deacon settled between her thighs and rubbed the head of his cock over her pearl. She gasped and arched her back, bumping against the source of pleasure.

"Want me?" he teased, coating his hard length in her wet heat.

"Yes," she grabbed him by the rump and took control, lining up cock to cunny before he thrust home. Her orgasm began immediately and her channel flexed, squeezing and stroking his cock as she came. Her release triggered his and he plunged in and out with jarring thrusts, filling her with his seed.

As his release pulsed into her she wrapped her legs around his waist, sealing them together. Spent and exhausted, he managed to roll sideways before he collapsed. Afterward, with Miri's head on his shoulder and her body cuddled close, he let his mind wander through bliss and back to business.

"It's a damn shame we're leaving the crime boss at large." He sighed, reluctantly turning from passion to criminals.

"Minus his plates," Miri reminded him.

"That'll definitely make huge inroads in the counterfeiting business in Texas," he muttered. "I don't suppose Ned left a clue to the identity of the gang leader."

"I imagine he'll use the name to bargain for his freedom out of jail."

"Until then, Doyle said the plates were worth four times what Ned brought in and that's a nice tidy sum to tide us over while we puzzle out how to catch the leader."

Deacon figured Miri was right about Ned parlaying his information into a ticket out of jail, but it irritated him just the same. "Guess we best get this show on the road. Are you hungry?" He'd have rather curled up with her and slept the night, but they still had work to do.

"Yep," she answered. "It's back to being female for me."

She moved quickly in spite of her grumbled words, throwing open the closet to begin assembling her costume. That's how she described her outfits. Deacon understood the real Miri was the woman he'd just held in his arms and he didn't care what she wore or who she pretended to be in between.

After she finished packing their trunk, she appeared at his shoulder where he stood in front of the mirror knotting his tie.

"How do I look?" she asked, twirling around to give him an eyeful of goddess.

"You go from being a country bumpkin to a butler, to an old lady, to the beautiful woman standing before me. I don't know how you do it, sweetheart." He shook his head in wonder.

Plying her fan, she tapped his arm and batted her eyelashes at him.

"If ya don't give people a reason to doubt ya, they don't look close." She ruined the effect of the costume when she answered in Beau's Tennessee twang.

"See what I mean?" she asked, switching to the husky Southern accent that stroked Deacon's nerve endings.

"Trust me, in that getup, both men and women will be looking at you even if you bray like a jackass," Deacon growled, enjoying the hint of pink his observation brought to her cheeks. She stood in front of the mirror admiring the purple fabric that could have made a lesser woman look washed-out but enhanced Miri's Amazonian beauty.

"Hiram's lady friend is amazing. She sewed the pouches and pockets in this dress just like I asked."

"*You* are amazing," he answered and she flashed him a wicked grin, turning toward him but peering over her shoulder at her image one last time. It didn't escape Deacon's notice that his wife preened like a peacock when she wore her new finery.

On the way to the dining hall, Deacon and Miri stopped at the front desk, arranging for their baggage to be carried to the stage depot for transport back to Eclipse. With her tall stature, fulsome breasts, exotic eyes and silver hair, Miri was breathtaking and unforgettable.

Deacon recognized the way other men coveted Miri. Usually he wondered if he'd been fair, scooping her up before anyone else discovered the secret woman beneath her disguise. This time though, he remembered her fierce declaration of love for him and did his own preening. *She's mine.*

While she went on to the room, he brought the horses to the back of the hotel and waited for Beauregard. When Miri didn't join him disguised or otherwise, Deacon left the horses tethered and returned to the hotel room.

* * * * *

Preparing for the ride back to Eclipse, Miri changed into her buckskins. Glad for the layers of male clothing, she discarded her female costume and assembled her Beauregard disguise, mindful of the coming cold.

She looked forward to the trip with Deacon and it had begun to seem to her as if she'd never get her fill of being with him. *He loves me.* She sighed. She couldn't quite believe in all this yet. She'd never said *I love you* to anyone before unless she counted Possum and Ketchum. But she knew even before they'd exchanged their closet vows, she'd been plumb simple-silly over Deacon.

It hadn't taken her but a moment to decide she liked partnering with him. She worried some she wouldn't last in his affections and decided she'd do her best to carry her own weight.

That's why she decided to get the hang of tasting his man parts. She loved it when he pleasured her that way and from his reaction earlier in the day to her awkward attempts, she could see he'd enjoy it just the same.

She wanted him to crave her as much as she wanted him. She knew she'd gotten the better part of the deal. Aside from Possum and Ketchum — and they weren't possessions as much as friends — she didn't own squat.

The only thing Deacon got with Miri was a new roof on his cabin by the river and her — but he seemed real certain that was enough. He'd not tarried, simplifying her transition from being bounty hunter Beau Beauregard to wife Miri McCallister.

When she'd told him straight out that she didn't know how women acted or dressed, he'd helped her with her female wardrobe, steering her to the women's clothes at the CQ Mercantile.

Deacon had ignored the scandalized clerk when he'd stood with Miri in the unmentionables section, discussing cotton drawers versus silk pantalettes. Seeing that the older woman was about to have a fit of the vapors, Miri had urged him over to the ranch supplies.

"See, nothing to it," he'd murmured, winked at Miri, turned to the clerk, tipped his hat and departed. Miri had been well pleased that although the store employee had sold Beau honey many times, she didn't recognize Miri McCallister as the same person.

When she'd come away with cotton drawers and no dresses, he'd listened again.

"Deacon, I can't run in skirts, nor kick, nor defend myself. If women dressed right, I'd be willing. But the way those skirts drag and the corset squeezes the breath out of me, why that's plumb stupid. I won't do it." She'd been militant and defiant.

He'd scratched his jaw, considering her words, thinking about the problem not her anger. He was smart that way.

"We'll talk to Hiram's lady friend, Roberta Harris. She owns Tailored Dreams, a millinery and sewing shop here in town."

He hadn't waited for her agreement. He'd simply taken her arm and guided her to the shop.

Inside, Miss Harris had provided a thick book filled with pictures and they'd all sat at a table studying the sketches. He'd made every decision easy until the only hard part had been standing still to be measured. By the end of the session, Miri called her Roberta and they'd gotten cozy, exchanging gossip about Eclipse citizens. Deacon had disappeared.

The next trip to town, he'd left after he'd escorted her to Tailored Dreams to pick up her first outfit. "I'll be back after I talk to Hiram."

She'd stood in front of the mirror, gawking at the fashionable woman wearing a split riding skirt, white ruffled shirtwaist, vest, leather boots and a flat-brimmed hat. It was amazing. She knew it was her, but it wasn't. She'd been trying to get used to her appearance when the bell on the entrance announced Deacon's return.

When he'd opened the door to the fitting room she'd been smoothing her hand over the vest, studying the swell of her breasts under the ruffled shirt. He'd stalled in the doorway, a splash of red staining his cheekbones. He'd been quiet on the way home and ferocious in his lovemaking when they arrived.

"Well, thanks to Deacon, I'm getting plenty of practice being female." Miri grimaced and then grinned at her Beauregard disguise reflected in the mirror.

She didn't doubt that Deacon would use their current case to get more detective business. She didn't mind letting him direct things. Though his methodical approach to planning ventures was different from her spur-of-the-moment decisions, when they compared ideas, their end conclusions were usually pretty much the same.

A quick search of their room confirmed that she'd left nothing behind. She wasn't surprised when a knock sounded. She swung open the door, expecting the arrival of the hotel porter to fetch their trunk downstairs for shipping. Instead, she faced Lydia Lynch accompanied by Adam Crispin.

"Well howdy-do," she drawled in her best Tennessee twang. "Sure wish I had a gun in hand instead of a tip for the hotel employee."

Crispin didn't have the same trouble. He held his derringer pointing at her heart.

"Beau, I want my brother," Lydia said as soon as she stepped through the door, Crispin following.

"What's his interest in Ned?" Miri asked, nodding at Lydia's companion.

"I want my plates, you little cocksucker," he snarled.

"Well, all righty then. Guess the only thing left to know, Miss Lynch, is if you took part in the counterfeiting business while you were running the Pleasure Dome."

Miri addressed her question to the brothel owner but kept her gaze on Crispin's gun.

Deacon eased his grip from the knob, leaning closer to the door to better hear the murmur of voices on the other side — definitely more than one. The porter coming down the hall pushing a luggage cart before him gave Deacon what he needed.

Wearing the old man's hat and jacket, he knocked at the suite, then hunched over the cart, keeping his head low as the door swung open.

"Here to pick up the trunk," he muttered, wheeling the cart before him.

Two steps into the room, he shoved it as if it were a battering ram, knocking Adam Crispin to the floor. Deacon jumped him, wrestling for the gun in the gambler's hand.

"Oh no you don't," Miri said in Beau's voice, blocking Lydia's move toward the exit.

Deacon stood, pulling Crispin with him to his feet and Miri cuffed Lydia's arms behind her.

"Good work, partner," she drawled. "Things were just gettin' interestin'. Crispin here wants his plates."

"Is that right? Guess this is our lucky day."

"Deacon, thank God you're here. I don't know anything about plates. I'm here because I need your help." The owner of the Pleasure Dome looked at him beseechingly.

"What do you want, Lydia?" Deacon asked. "More to the point, why are you with Crispin?"

"I came to beg you to help me free Ned." She glared at Miri. "You caused this mess when you posed as my butler. Now you can help fix it. "

"What's Crispin doin' with ya?" Miri drawled in Beau's voice.

"He offered to escort me here when I discovered Deacon was staying at the Ellis." She looked at Beau with disgust. "What are you doing here?"

"Lydia, meet my wife's cousin, Beau Beauregard," Deacon said before Miri responded.

"Don't be stupid, Deacon. I knew all of Annie's relatives and this bumpkin is no relative of hers."

"My present wife is in the salon below, waiting for me to join her," Deacon corrected Lydia. "We're

314

here on our honeymoon. Now maybe you'd like to explain why you're here with the head of the counterfeiting ring. On the other hand, Beau and I should thank you. We won't have to track Crispin now."

Lydia glared at Crispin, then turned to Deacon. "I need to get back to my house. I don't know what Adam is involved—"

"Shut up, Lydia," Crispin snarled before she could say anything that might incriminate him further or reveal where she stood in the counterfeiting business.

The fact that the madam closed her mouth at his order told its own tale about her involvement.

"Lydia, you can tell your story to the U.S. marshal. Crispin, I'm sure the Fort Worth sheriff will be pleased as punch to have company." He looked at Miri and smiled grimly. "Ready, Beau?"

Epilogue

Christmas, 1885

"Who pledges to guide this child in the ways of the Great Spirit in the Sky?" Robert McCallister bent over Samuel Elliot McCallister, Jr., smoothing the fluffy blond hair on the baby's head.

"His mama and I do," Sam said gruffly. The idea of Snake McCallister, reformed whoremonger and retired killer, making the commitment would have been ludicrous if the vow hadn't been delivered with such conviction.

Deacon's throat tightened at the aura of love surrounding Sam and his family. He spoke the words over Charles Wolf McCallister, Jr., and Charlie and Naomi held their son and pledged to guide Wolf on the path of a true warrior.

317

Granted, Deacon improvised with the christening, delivering it in words that embraced the complexities of both the Indian and white spirit worlds. But that didn't make the occasion any less solemn or real.

When the last baptism candidate stood before him, Deacon touched Miri's forehead with a drop of the mountain water Charlie had fetched from the purest stream.

"And do you, Miracle Beauregard McCallister, accept me as your guide and teacher as I accept the miracle of you. Will you follow the path to the Source of all Knowledge as we learn the way together?"

Her nod was jerky, her whispered acceptance a husky, "Yes."

Deacon settled the white shawl around her shoulders, much as he'd wrapped each baby in a christening blanket. "May we all walk in the path of truth and leave treachery and discord behind."

Later, Miri swore she'd felt a tingle of warmth brush over her as Deacon said his words. Ketchum had rumbled a deep response in his throat as if he felt an otherworldly touch too.

After the christenings, the gift-giving and another slice each of Eden's apple pie, Miri sat in the front room of the McCallister house, surrounded by family as the end of Christmas 1884 drew near.

Deacon met her gaze and winked, making her grin.

"It was a mighty fine year, partner," she drawled in Beauregard's voice, a persona she like to don when emotion threatened to overwhelm her.

"Only the first of many, wife," Deacon answered, crossing the room to hug her to his side.

Because of the late hour, the knock on the front door startled all of them. Deacon left the front room with Charlie and Sam close behind. The Eclipse sheriff stood with two other people on the porch when the McCallisters opened the door.

"Merry Christmas, Hiram. Always a pleasure to see you," Deacon greeted him.

Ketchum, wearing a holiday bow, growled softly as he took his place beside in the line of McCallister males.

"You're back," Miri whooped and skidded across the floor, flinging her arms around Hiram for a bear hug.

"Yep, and brought you a present." He nodded at the man and woman standing behind him.

"Ben, Laura?"

Deacon waited as Miri hugged the woman and pumped the man's hand, then turned to him with an introduction.

"This is my husband, Robert McCallister. Deacon, these are my friends who run the Hearth and Home. We met back when we were all strays left to grow up in the Tennessee Home for Foundlings and Orphans. Why we've known each other..." Whatever else she had been going to say, her welcoming expression changed to puzzlement and her words piddled to a halt.

"What might you folks be doing away from the orphanage on Christmas Eve?" As he asked, Deacon held Miri's hand, entwining her fingers with his.

The woman named Laura began to cry, Ben looked belligerent and then crumbled as Hiram revealed what they'd been up to.

"The crate you sent came back on the stage. I asked the driver, Conner Spokes about it. He said it being an orphanage and you wanting them to get their presents, he tried to make delivery. When he couldn't find it, he asked around. There is no Hearth and Home for Orphans and Foundlings."

"Well that can't be right. Mr. Stokes must have gotten confused." Ben and Laura flinched under the evidence of Miri's trust.

Hiram shook his head grimly. "Nope. I wired the Dyer County Sheriff in Tennessee and he met me when I got into town. We decided to personally check on those orphans you've been paying for. Imagine our surprise when the Hearth and Home turned out to be a fancy hotel."

Clearly Hiram didn't want to deliver the information, but he did just the same. Ben and Laura didn't bother with a denial.

"All that money you supplied for the schooling, feeding and day-to-day tending of seven children ranging in age from three to twelve—there is no Bobbi, Alice, Jeannie, Jimmy, Caroline, Lollie or Seth. You've been investing in a mighty nice hotel. I brought these two along because if you didn't hear it from the miscreants themselves, I knew you'd never believe you've been swindled."

Deacon didn't expect Miri to cry or show her upset, but he didn't expect her to laugh either.

"No kids, huh?" She skewered Laura with a shrewd look. "I bet this was your idea, wasn't it? You always were good at laying out a plan and following through."

Miri seemed completely unperturbed when she escorted her two former friends to the kitchen where she served them pie and coffee.

"You're in charge of her now, McCallister. I can quit worrying." Hiram settled down with his dessert, listening to the story Ben and Laura told. According to them, they'd seen the hotel as a grand investment of Miri's money. They, of course, had intended to tell her the truth, but hadn't gotten around to it.

"You were so excited about the children, I didn't want to tell you the way of it and let you down." A fat tear trickled down the woman's cheek and Deacon felt momentary sympathy.

"Forget about the tears. As I recall, you could turn them on and off." Miri laughed again.

Deacon decided Miri had her old friend pegged right, because the tears evaporated as soon as it was clear they wouldn't buy any sympathy.

"We need to get back," Ben muttered, glaring at Hiram. "We had to leave the manager in charge."

"A manager, huh?" Miri went into peals of laughter again and Deacon worried that maybe she was hysterical. But when she sobered up, she said slyly, "Me and my husband will have a look at the books come the first of the year. Sounds like we own a fair share of the hotel. Wouldn't that be right, Deacon?"

"Yep. And Hiram says it's right smack in the middle of town, with twenty-five rooms to let."

"The Dryer County sheriff says they keep 'em full most of the time." Hiram poured a second cup of coffee and leaned back, studying the two.

"We have worked hard to build —" Laura began defensively.

"Using my wife's money," Deacon cut off her excuse.

"A third each," Ben offered. "Our work should count for —"

"Half," Miri said and smiled. "I appreciate your labor. But I worked hard too to get you the money."

"Are you going to have us arrested?" Laura asked tensely.

"Naw," Miri answered and let Deacon draw her out of the room. "Best not tarry long in Eclipse. You've got a business to keep running so my investment wasn't for naught."

She even stood in the doorway and called after them, "Merry Christmas" when Hiram ushered them back into the night. Before he left, he said he'd let the law know about the new ownership details.

Instead of traveling back to their cabin by the river, Deacon and Miri elected to stay over and have breakfast with the rest of the McCallister family. The women had decreed it a new tradition, an idea that warmed Deacon's heart in places he'd not realized were cold.

His former bedroom lacked the warmth of Annie's cabin and he almost regretted staying over. It also lacked privacy. He propped a chair against the bedroom door to keep it shut and divested himself of his clothes, but Miri beat him in her disrobing and jumped in the bed first.

"I 'spect you think I'm a ninny," she said self-consciously, sitting in the bed with her knees drawn up, staring at him.

"Nope," he answered smugly. "I think you're a force of nature, a gift from God to Laura and Ben as well as me. I think you're a miracle." He slid under the blanket and pulled her into his arms, nuzzling her behind the ear until she dissolved into giggles.

"I love you, Deacon Robert McCallister," she whispered. "Don't take on about the kids. I reckon we'll have our own young'uns someday."

Deacon didn't explain that he'd developed no fond yearnings for seven unknown youngsters. Instead he settled next to her, leaving the lamp on as he handed her the paper Hiram had left behind.

Miri unfolded the letter, scanning the contents, and Deacon watched her expression change from curious to ecstatic. The letter identified Miri and Robert McCallister as legal agents of the state of Texas.

"It's stretching the truth a mite, isn't it?" she asked cautiously.

"Nope. Hiram said he cleared it with Logan Doyle before he wrote it. The state bankers and lawmen are grateful for us bringing in the counterfeiters and stolen plates."

"Well, I reckon we've got some detecting to do then, partner. Where to next, preacher man?"

"Anywhere is home when I'm with you, Mrs. McCallister." Deacon pulled Miri into his embrace and settled himself between her thighs. "I'll love you forever, sweetheart," he whispered before sliding deep inside her wet heat, where he needed to be.

The End

More Books by Gem Sivad

Historical Westerns

Eclipse Heat series:

Quincy's Woman

Intimate Strangers

Wolf's Tender

Tupelo Gold

Five Card Stud

Breed True

Trouble in Disguise

Whispering Grace

Unlikely Gentlemen series:

River's Edge

Outrageous Pride

Cerise Amour

Stand Alone Titles:

Staged Affair

Pinch of Naughty

Historical Paranormal

Jinx series:

Cat Nip

Blood Stoned

Contemporary Paranormal

Bitter Creek Holler series:

Call Me Miz

Miz Spelled

Ursus Horribilis

Contemporary Romantic Suspense

Smoke, Inc. series

Cowboy Burn—Ring in a Cowboy Anthology

Rhythm—2016

A note from the author...

Hi. I'm Gem Sivad. Nice to meet you. If you're reading this, you probably just finished one of my books. I write paranormal, contemporary, and historical romance. Whichever genre you sampled, I hope you enjoyed.

Although I have hermit tendencies, occasionally I venture out of the writer's den to meet readers at book signing events. In case we don't connect in person, you can find Gem Sivad at the cyber locations below.

For book release updates (or if you're an avid Words with Friends junkie like I am) play with me on Facebook @ facebook.com/GemSivadAuthor.

Visit my website @ gemsivad.com for snippets from the current works in progress. And of course, never miss a Gem Sivad contest or giveaway by subscribing to Dreamcatcher newsletter:
Dreamcatcher Newsletter @ http://gemsivad.com/subscribe/

Happy reading,
Gem Sivad

Made in the USA
Charleston, SC
15 June 2016